VACATION AT SAN PEDRO

By the same author

Bad News from Espera

Vacation at San Pedro

D.A. HORNCASTLE

ROBERT HALE · LONDON

© D.A. Horncastle 1993
First published in Great Britain 1993

ISBN 0 7090 4972 2

Robert Hale Limited
Clerkenwell House
Clerkenwell Green
London EC1R 0HT

The right of D.A. Horncastle to be identified as
author of this work has been asserted by him
in accordance with the Copyright, Designs and
Patents Act 1988.

For Julie

Photoset in North Wales by
Derek Doyle & Associates, Mold, Clwyd.
Printed and bound in Great Britain by
WBC Print Ltd, and WBC Bookbinders Ltd,
Bridgend, Mid-Glamorgan.

ONE

'Hiya, Brad!'

As he opened the door of the rail car, a broad smile creased his face. He'd recognize that Texas drawl anywhere.

Beth jumped down from the buckboard she'd parked in the shade of a trackside warehouse and ran across the parallel set of rails towards him, her rangy strides raising miniature clouds of dust in the noonday heat.

'Brad it's bin such a long time ...'

They paused in a brief moment of embarrassed mutual appraisal. Then with a whoop of delight she slammed into his open arms, almost knocking him off balance.

'She's my sister,' he felt obliged to tell the grizzled conductor when he had finally disentangled himself.

'Shore ain't no business o' mine, mister.' The man's mouth widened into a gap-toothed grin. He had the world-weary air of a man used to seeing a multitude of greetings and leavings.

Beth stopped rubbing her head on Brad's chest and let him go. As he stooped to pick up his bag he caught sight of the row of faces grinning down at them from the rail car, the stifling heat and boredom of the long journey north from Austin relieved by this heartwarming interlude.

Beth grabbed Brad's hand, oblivious to everyone. 'C'mon shake a leg, the Double Circle is only an hour outa town. Then your vacation really starts!' She whooped and hugged him again. 'Brad, I still cain't believe it! Is it really you! After all these years – we sure got some catchin' up to do.'

Brad grinned as he tossed his bag on to the buckboard. Same old Beth, always bustling round, never happy unless she was bossing people. As he handed her up into the seat, she grabbed the reins – nobody drove Beth.

'I guess you don't even know Tom and I have got two kids,' Beth said as she flicked the whip expertly across the flanks of the roan. 'But then, I never had chance to tell you I'd gotten hitched, not knowin' where you were. Say, how does it feel to be Uncle Brad?'

Brad winced at the reproach in her voice. Not knowing for sure whether he was alive or dead, must have been hell for her. But their separation was just one of the minor tragedies of a war that had affected so many lives.

'Hup, hup!' The roan flicked his ears at Beth's sharp command. They had left the last isolated houses of San Pedro behind them. The train whistled mournfully as it left the depot and trundled alongside them. As the locomotive hissed and belched steam, the roan wanted no further encouragement to break into a steady, mile-eating lope.

'We don't never lose touch again, ya hear?' Beth chided him. 'Why, iffen we hadn't read about that fracas down Espera way, I'd have never known I could find you through Captain McNelly.'

She was in that tight-lipped, telling off mood. But deep down he knew he'd take all the stick she handed out, for he damn well deserved it. He looked at her, a smile in his eyes, taking in the lean, raw-boned features that made her look even more attractive now she was older. One day, maybe he'd find a girl as open and kind as Beth.

'You hearing me?'

He grinned sheepishly. 'I hear you.'

She eyed him speculatively. 'You ain't changed, have you? Never did have much to say. But I know you, Brad Saunders, you run deeper than most. Ain't you never gonna say you're sorry 'bout what you did to me?'

'What can I say? You know I had to join up, Beth. After Clem got killed I was all burned up inside.'

Her blue eyes softened. 'Oh, Brad, I understood. You worshipped Clem. What hurt was the way you just upped and went. You left me high an' dry with nary a note – but then you weren't the writin' kind.'

'I couldn't bring myself to tell you. You would have done your dangdest to stop me, you know that.'

She looked him full in the face. 'Ferget it. It's all in the past. I got you back again, that's all that matters. Now I guess there's somethin' I gotta tell you.'

For once Beth was hesitant. 'You'll like Tom,

he's a good man but ... aw, you gotta know sooner or later – he was a gen'ral.'

Brad's eyebrows raised a fraction. 'So? You married well; I'm real pleased fer you, Beth.'

She gazed at him, a defiant look in her blue eyes. 'Sure he was a gen'ral, Brad – *in the Union Army!*'

They fell silent for a moment.

'You got anything to say about that – say it right now, ya hear?'

Brad looked away. If Beth had told him ten years ago that she'd married a carpetbagger, ex-Union general or no, he'd have walked out on her. 'Beth, I got nuthin' to say and that's the honest truth. Your happiness is what counts. I'm real sorry 'bout what I did ...'

She stopped him with a look. 'I done told you – don't apologize. We were both bred from the same stock. Pa was as contrary as an old steer that's never been branded.'

Brad looked at her quizzically. 'How come you came out thisaway?'

'Well, after you quit, I guess I couldn't settle. The war had took Clem and fer all I knew, you, too. I quit schoolmarmin' and went nursing.' She shot him a glance that took him apart. 'I was with Lee's army at Antietam.'

Brad stared at his sister. 'I was there, too – ridin' with Jeb Stuart on Nicodemus Hill.'

'There you go,' Beth replied. 'So we weren't so far apart after all, were we? I'm sure glad you didn't end up in hospital all shot up like Tom.'

He bit his lip. 'Antietam was the bloodiest day's fightin' I ever saw.'

Beth's face turned sombre. 'Thank God I didn't know you were there – they were bringin' in you butternuts by the cartload. I guess I aged ten years that day. But that's enough of reminiscin'.' She looked at him with pride. 'Hey, hey! So I got me a real live Texas Ranger fer a brother! Now how about that? The kids cain't wait to meet you.' Her expression changed from banter to one of concern. She cast a clinical eye at Brad. 'You need some meat on them bones. No wonder Captain McNelly didn't argue when I wrote and suggested you take a vacation.'

'So it was you who prompted him?'

'Sure – an' you know me, I don't take no fer an answer.'

'How's Tom?' Brad made a valiant effort to change the subject.

'My Tom? I gotta tell you, Brad. I'm real proud of him. He's standing for mayor.'

She looked radiant. Brad felt a glow of pleasure. At last she was truly happy – it was no more than her due.

The horse caught the scent of home and the wheels of the buckboard raised a cloud of dust as they clattered along the winding trail that ran beside a river which cut through hilly terrain, thickly forested with oak.

'So what's with this ranger business?' Beth glanced at him quizzically. 'Ain't you had your fill of fightin'? McNelly mentioned your war record when he replied to my letter. He thinks highly of you. But you cain't take on the whole world, Brad.' She waved a slim hand. 'There's too many mean cusses out there. It's high time you found yourself a wife and settled down.'

'I never got round to that, I guess.'

Beth smiled and patted his arm. 'Don't worry, none, we got one or two real lookers round here. Why, there's Tom's sister, Janelle – she's come over from New York to stop by with us. Her husband owned an ironworks back east. He died six months ago. She's a real eye-catchin' woman – and wealthy, too.'

She paused as two riders appeared on the crest of a low hill ahead on the trail. Brad instinctively moved his right hand cautiously to his hip, grimacing as he realized his Colt was packed away with his gear. After all, he wasn't looking for trouble, he was here on vacation.

If Beth had noticed his precautionary movement, she didn't remark upon it. 'It must be the kids!' she exclaimed.

She flicked the whip. The roan put her head down and hammered along the trail. As the two riders edged down off the hill to intercept them, Brad felt a twinge of misgiving. Even at that distance the difference in size between men and children was perfectly clear. The glint of sun from a gun barrel cinched it.

He glanced round. His bag lay on the floor of the buckboard, way out of reach. It was too late anyway; Beth had already caught sight of the two riders. Their heavily masked faces produced a typical reaction from her. The whip coiled back and she drove the roan straight at them as they straddled the trail, forcing them to part company, their horses rearing in alarm as the buckboard shot between them.

It ain't no use, thought Brad as he backvaulted into the well of the buckboard, one hand grasping for his bag.

He was right. He had scarcely opened the first buckle before a slug whined overhead.

That was just a warning. Beth lashed the whip at the flanks of the lathered roan in a desperate attempt to get away.

He was right again, for the next shot went clean through the head of the roan, dropping the animal dead in a long slithering slide on the dusty track.

The buckboard overturned with a grinding crash. Brad felt himself hurtling through the air before he hit the ground with a jolt that made his teeth chatter.

As he raised himself on his elbow, the sounds of two horses drawing near at a steady clop drew his attention. The men approaching were obviously in no hurry for they had achieved their objective.

Mindful of two Winchesters pointing at him, Brad struggled to his feet. A searing pain knifed deep into his right shoulder, making him grunt with agony. He tested it gingerly and winced. He must have put it out.

Where was Beth? He looked round anxiously. She was lying face down, about twenty yards away.

'Stay right there!' a voice commanded as he made to approach her.

He looked up as the two riders trotted close, searching for some clue to their identity. But the gunny sacks pulled over their heads made facial description impossible. They wore stetsons with huge crowns, vests over sweat-stained check shirts and faded levis.

Brad was under no illusions. These men were outlaws. What the hell did they want with him and Beth?

'We ain't carrying any money,' he offered.

The two men guffawed.

'It ain't *yore* money we're after,' one of them said.

His partner seemed to see a certain humour in the remark, for he snickered approval. He dismounted and approached Beth who still lay unconscious.

'Check her out,' the man remaining on horseback said. 'She ain't no use dead.'

As he slid the Winchester back into its scabbard and drew a Colt, Brad's keen glance noticed that the back of his hand carried a tattoo.

'Sure, sure,' his companion replied.

Brad noted how he moved with the alacrity of a young man as he bent over Beth and placed his hands round the neck of her dress. In one movement he ripped the dress open to the waist.

'Hold it right there!' the horseman said as Brad started forward. As the man brought up his gun, Brad caught a clear sight of the tattoo on the back of his wrist – it was of a coiled rattlesnake, just about to strike.

'My, ain't she just all woman!' His sidekick bent over Beth, his eyes leering at her before he bent to put his ear to her naked breasts.

Brad instinctively averted his eyes, feeling his gorge rise at the totally unnecessary violation of his sister's modesty.

'C'mon, don't take all day!' the horseman snapped.

The other man stood up. 'She'll live,' he said cynically. 'If only long enough for me to ...'

'Shut up!' The man on horseback never took his eyes off Brad as he spoke. 'We ain't got time fer that. Now quit lustin' over her and get her across my hoss.'

'What's with all this?' Brad demanded. 'She's my sister. Tom Anderson's wife. He's the boss of the Double Circle. There'll be hell to pay when this gets out.'

The horseman nodded. By now he had Beth draped across his saddle. Brad felt his anger rising to boiling point.

'Reckon yore right there,' said the horseman. 'You don't interest me. But Mr General Anderson does. And it won't be hell he's paying.'

His companion sniggered.

Brad took a few steps forward. His shoulder protested with pain, but he paid no need. Commonsense was one thing, but there was no way he could let these two ride off with Beth. It was time to play his only card. 'Now just hold it, you guys, I guess there's somethin' you don't know,' he said.

The second man was mounted now. They faced him, saying nothing.

'Well, now, see here, boys, I'm a Texas Ranger.'

Both men burst into a shout of laughter.

'Hell now, ain't that just the funniest thing?' said the one carrying Beth. 'Every hustler from here to the Mexican border claims he's a ranger. Iffen it's true, Texas must be crawling with 'em. Next thing is you'll be telling us you work for McNelly's bunch.'

Brad raised his left hand towards his vest, intending to display the badge that proclaimed his office.

'Let's see him dance,' said one of the men. He cocked and deliberately aimed his weapon, emptying it systematically at Brad's feet, forcing him to do an ungainly series of hops to avoid the barrage of slugs. All the while, the outlaw whooped and roared with laughter.

As the chamber clicked empty, Brad made a rush forward. The barrel of the other man's gun was trained on him, but Brad didn't care. He had only one thought on his mind, to save his beloved Beth from this shameful abduction.

His sudden movement caused both riders' mounts to shy and rear.

Head down, Brad never saw the outlaw trigger off a shot in his direction. All he felt was a heavy blow, followed by a searing pain in his scalp before he collapsed in a heap on the track beside the overturned buckboard.

TWO

By the time they came to a halt, Beth was thoroughly shaken by her bruising ride.

Throughout the journey she had no idea of where they were heading, for a filthy, sweat-stained bandanna had been tied round her face, masking it completely from the clouds of choking dust flung up by the horses' hooves. They seemed to have been on the move for hours, constantly changing direction, until it dawned on her that her captors were taking immense trouble to cover their tracks.

What had happened to Brad? Lying unconscious on the ground after the heavy fall from the buckboard, she had no idea of what had happened to Brad. A sudden feeling of panic seized her. Was he still alive?

'Take her down and shove her inside, Billy Boy.' It was the older man sitting astride the horse which carried her who spoke. All through the long ride, Beth had marked him as the one who gave the orders.

'Hey, Joe, she's across your hoss,' the younger man objected, a note of juvenile belligerence in his high-pitched voice.

'Jest do it.'

Reluctantly, Billy Boy dismounted. He was none too particular about the way he handled Beth as he pushed her off the horse.

With an effort, she scrambled to her feet. Her hands were tied in front of her and she held them up across the torn bodice of her dress, in an effort to preserve her modesty. She managed to pull the bandanna clear of her face and looked wildly about her, trying desperately to find something to place this location in relation to the Double Circle in her disorientated mind.

To her intense disappointment she recognized nothing. They were standing outside what appeared to be a disused barn in the middle of a forest glade.

Both her captors removed the gunny sacks which concealed their faces. Used as she was to seeing all types of men, she found it difficult to conceal her revulsion. A rougher pair than this she had never seen, even among the casuals who came riding by the ranch, looking for temporary work.

The sun-reddened skin of Billy Boy's face was sprouting a two-day old stubble. His narrow forehead and broken nose gave him an ape-like appearance enhanced by his barrel-like chest, long arms and short legs. His only redeeming feature was the corn yellow hair which tumbled on to his squat shoulders as lightly as any woman's.

The older man was taller and decidedly less heavily built than his companion but there was a certain cat-like litheness about his movements. In contrast to the younger man's, his iron-grey hair was cropped short, giving him the appearance of a convict. But it was his eyes that repelled Beth – sunk deep in the sockets of his gaunt face, they were as cold and unwinking as those of the striking rattlesnake tattooed prominently on his right wrist.

Beth gave an involuntary shudder when she saw the tattoo. She did her best to avoid looking directly at this man, for the look in his eyes made her feel uneasy. Somehow she could not rid herself of the feeling that she had seen him somewhere before ...

But Beth had no intention of submitting meekly to these two men. 'Just what do you think you two are doin'?' she demanded. 'Where's my brother?'

When neither of the men answered her question, she stood her ground. 'Can't you tell me at least why I have been abducted like this?'

Billy Boy lifted his hat and scratched his head reflectively. 'I don't rightly know what you mean, ma'am,' he said.

The older man sighed. 'Didn't you get no schoolin', knucklehead? She's asking why we've brought her here.'

Billy Boy guffawed. 'Well, now, why didn't you say so? Say, Joe, what do we do now?'

Beth didn't like the unpleasant way Billy Boy looked at her as he spoke.

'Now, see here, my brother is a Texas Ranger ...' Beth began.

The older man grinned, showing a row of teeth as blackened as a row of ageing tombstones. 'So he said,' he said callously.

Beth tried to control the rising tide of panic inside her. 'You ... you didn't kill him?' she whispered.

'I reckon Billy Boy had a darned good try.'

'I told you – he's a Texas Ranger.'

The older man turned to stare at her. 'Well, now ma'am, is that a fact?'

'Too bad.' Billy Boy's high-pitched laugh followed his remark.

'He wasn't armed,' Beth said quietly. 'When Captain McNelly finds out what you've done, your lives won't be worth a candle.'

'Shut yore mouth!' Joe shouted. 'We'll be long gone before he gets here.' He glanced at the sun and then walked over to his horse, fished in the saddle-bag and produced a large envelope. His eyes flashed in a predatory gleam. 'I need to find someplace to fix this,' he said. 'Someplace where one of the Double Circle cowpokes will find it. I'm gonna have to leave you here with the woman, Billy Boy. But no interferin' with her, ya hear?'

'I hear you, Joe, but say, I saw her first ...'

Billy Boy's words died in a gargle as his companion stepped forward and seized him by the throat. 'Billy Boy, you wanna ride with me, you do as I say. While ever she's in one piece she's worth every cent of this fifty thousand dollars we're askin'. Jest shove that into yore thick skull an' keep it there.'

Beth shrank back into the shadow cast by the dilapidated barn. Fifty thousand dollars! The very thought made her feel faint. 'But ... but ... Tom don't have that kinda money,' she whispered. 'The cattle business is goin' through a bad time, all his

Vacation at San Pedro

money is tied up in the ranch.'

Joe laughed. 'That ain't my problem.' He tapped the envelope with his forefinger. 'So General Anderson is short of greenbacks, is he? Well, that goes for all of us. I guess he's gonna soon find out who his friends really are.'

'What have you got against my husband?' Beth pleaded.

Joe laughed harshly. 'You ain't recognized me, have you? I'm Joe Levine.'

'Joe Levine?' Beth gasped.

'That's right. Changed a bit, haven't I?' He moved closer to Beth until his face was barely inches away. 'Take a good long look, Mrs Anderson. That's what five years in Austin Penitentiary does to a man and it's all down to a lousy carpetbagger.'

Beth held his gaze. 'You got what you deserved.'

There was a crack as Levine struck Beth a vicious backhander across the face.

He took hold of Beth and came in so close she could smell the stale odour on his breath. 'But I'll tell you this, Mrs Anderson, I'm gonna get what's due to me outa this, an' that's a promise.'

Beth did not reply. She'd heard enough to realize that to say more would only provoke Levine into more violence.

Levine strode towards his horse. 'I'm leavin', now,' he announced.

Beth fell prey to an overwhelming sense of desperation. While the two men were together, she sensed relative safety, but the thought of being left alone with the grinning, half-wit called Billy Boy was more than she could bear. The spectacle of the two outlaws quarrelling over her gave life to her legs. She jumped to her feet and, knocking Levine off-balance as she rushed past him, she started to run as fast as she could.

'Hey, whoa there!'

The startled shouts of the two men combined as they broke off their argument and set off in pursuit.

It was no contest. Hampered by her hands, still tied together in front of her, Beth had stumbled and fallen on the trackless terrain before she had gone fifty yards. She struggled gamely to her feet, but by the time Billy Boy caught up with her on top of a slope, she realized she was deep in an oak forest on the side of a rugged hill, far from any other form of habitation. It was useless to resist, plainly there was nowhere to go.

Billy Boy's thickset body floored her with a heavy tackle. He lingered on top of Beth longer than was necessary until the older man arrived and hauled him to his feet by the scruff of his neck.

'That wasn't smart, ma'am,' Levine told her. 'It means we'll have to keep a real sharp eye on you from now on.'

They frog-marched her into the barn and thrust her inside. As they entered a slight scuffling noise caught their attention.

Beth froze.

'Hell, it's only a rat!' Billy Boy's high-pitched squeak of a laugh ran through Beth. Although a country girl bred and born she had never been able to abide rats.

She paused, trying to compose herself to face

this new horror as well as adjust to the musty smell and the dim light which was relieved by the odd shaft of sunlight slatting through gaps in the timbered roof.

'Better knee halter her, Billy Boy, that'll curb her roamin',' Levine said.

Billy Boy set to the task with obvious relish. He went back to his horse to fetch his lariat, cut off a length with his Bowie knife and secured Beth's ankles in a way that enabled her to walk only in an undignified hop.

'Ain't no man alive could undo that knot,' he bragged as he stepped back to survey his handiwork.

'I'm leavin' now,' Levine announced. 'I gotta fix this notice so it's read tomorrow. I'll overnight on the range. Tomorrow mornin' I'm ridin' into town.'

'What you gonna do that for?' demanded Billy Boy. 'Someone might spot you.'

Levine looked around him contemptuously. 'After five years? Anyway, we need supplies.' He paused beside the door. 'Now remember, Billy Boy, when I git back I wanna find the woman here in one piece. There's a heap of money ridin' on this and I don't wanna lose a cent through yore foolin'. Got it?'

Beth waited until he had gone. In the dim light, she could see Billy Boy fidgeting about. Plucking up courage she said, 'Billy Boy, what's your interest in all this? How come you're in with a man like him?'

'I met him in Austin,' Billy Boy said sullenly. 'He'd just finished doin' his time. He told me he was headin' this way and needed a sidekick fer this job he was pullin'.'

'Did he tell you why he was doin' this?'

'Do you think he tells me anything?' Billy Boy replied sullenly. 'All I know is that it's gonna cost your man dear to get you back.'

'So he's promised to pay you a share of the ransom?'

'I reckon so.'

'Billy Boy, you're too young to get involved with a man like Levine ...'

'Too young!' Billy Boy exploded. He slapped the Colt hanging low on his thigh. 'You wanna know somethin'? I done killed a man in Austin' cos he kept on callin' me Billy Boy.'

Beth fell silent.

Billy Boy uttered his high-pitched laugh. He puffed out his barrel-shaped chest as he strutted up and down the dimly lit barn. 'Yeah – I killed him. But the handle kinda stuck. I guess everyone calls me Billy Boy now. I reckon I got to like it.'

As Billy Boy smiled, almost genially, Beth realized that not only did he have homicidal tendencies, but he was also completely unpredictable. Putting these together with his immaturity, she realized she was in the custody of a young hoodlum with a lethal combination of traits in his warped personality.

She felt his gaze light on her. In one sudden movement he stepped forward and stripped away her torn dress, exposing her breasts.

'You sure are a good-lookin' woman, Mrs Anderson,' he said, almost shyly.

Beth knew that this moment was crucial; if she failed to stamp her personality on Billy Boy, the consequences did not bear thinking about. She must dominate him at all costs.

She raised her bound hands to cover her naked breasts and said, 'Billy Boy, is your ma still alive?'

'What you talkin' 'bout?'

'Son, I'm nigh old enough to be your ma. What would you say if this kinda thing happened to her?'

'I wouldn't say nuthin' I guess. Guess she was glad to see the back of me.' He turned away from Beth. 'Maybe she wasn't. Aw shucks, I'm gonna make me some coffee.'

Despite his glacial response, Beth thought she caught a hint of wistfulness in his voice. As she fumbled to rearrange her dress, she could only pray that by having pointed out the difference in their ages, she might be safe from his attention.

She began to feel safer by the minute as time passed and Billy Boy did not return. She had won this battle for the time being at least – but the other man, Joe Levine, was quite a different proposition ...

THREE

'Easy now!'

The sharp pain in his shoulder gutted him, but it was a woman's voice that gentled him. He lay still, bathed in perspiration, eyes still closed, aware of the softness of cool fingers on his forehead. For a moment he was transported back to childhood, when, sick of a fever, Beth had nursed him well again.

'Beth!' he croaked, for his mouth was so dry his tongue clove to the roof of his mouth.

'Shall we tell him?'

Through a haze in which weariness vied with pain and lost by a short head, Brad heard the woman speak. It was all he needed to focus his mind and have the memory of recent events come stampeding back.

With an effort he located the twin sources of his torment. His head throbbed. His shoulder ached, but when he stirred it, the agony he thought he might have felt had gone.

Beth!

Where the hell was Beth?

Suddenly he remembered everything with great clarity. He didn't want to believe it, but he would have needed a steel trap in his mind to shut it out.

'Shall I give him some water, Doctor?'

Once more the woman's voice troubled him. Who was it? Slowly, and with an effort that cost him more than he realized, he opened his eyes. Pinned tightly by the starched sheets, he caught a glimpse of rich blue velvet as the woman moved in closer, so close he could smell the musky smell of her.

'Beth?' His hopes rose as he spoke again, less huskily this time as the water that filled his mouth trickled smoothly down his burning throat.

'I'm not Beth,' came the reply. 'I'm her sister-in-law – Janelle.'

This time he opened his eyes and stared into the face of the woman. Her full lips curved in a smile as she looked down at him. Beyond her he saw the anxious face of a man.

'Brad, I'm Tom Anderson. Sorry we've had to meet under such harrowing circumstances. Doc Grierson's just put your shoulder back.'

A tall, gaunt man, around fifty years old, with a neatly clipped moustache and wings of grey hair flanking his forehead, his pale grey suit well cut, Tom Anderson spoke and looked like a former general. When he shifted his stance slightly, Brad saw he was resting on a stick.

Brad's eyes were fully open now, taking in the flower-patterned wallpaper, the framed watercolours on the wall and the vase of flowers standing on the sideboard. The floor must be carpeted for there was no noise as the coloured maid moved in the background with a man whom Brad took to be the doctor.

As Brad fingered the bandage round his head, the man stepped forward. 'You've got a slight graze on your scalp,' he told Brad. 'Your shoulder went back easy enough.'

'That all?'

'Together with the bruises, it's enough to keep you in bed for two or three days. Now, if you'll excuse me, I got a call to a sick child fifty miles from here.'

Tom Anderson waited while Doc Grierson left the room. Then he said, 'Brad, I gotta know what happened to Beth.'

'Leave him be, Tom, he isn't fit to think yet,' Janelle said.

Brad's head was clearing by the second. What had happened to Beth hadn't left him and never would. As long as he breathed, the two men who had abducted her were under the sentence of death.

With an effort he broke free from the constraint of the sheets and eased himself upright. The concerned faces of the two people in front of him came slowly into soft focus.

'Beth met me at the train depot. On the way back, two hombres waylaid us. They shot the hoss and took Beth,' he said sombrely.

'What reason would they have to do this?' asked Janelle.

'You tell me,' Brad replied.

'You gave them a fight by all accounts,' Tom said grimly.

Brad said nothing. To his dying day he would reckon he could have done more. But it was no use fretting over it. From this instant, every breathing moment was dedicated to getting Beth back.

He looked at Tom. 'How long have I been lying here?'

'Since late yesterday. My foreman rode out with a couple of the boys when you didn't show up. Said he found the busted buckboard and you lying beside it. No sign of Beth. Doc Grierson came as soon as he was able.'

Brad digested this. The slant of the sunlight through the window told him it was mid-morning. 'You heard anything yet?'

Tom shook his head.

'We need to talk some,' Brad said. 'I gotta know what lies behind this before I can act.'

'There ain't anything you can do Brad. You need rest. I've notified the sheriff. Meantime try to remember what you can.'

'Sure, sure, I'll take time out to talk with the sheriff.'

'That ain't what I mean, Brad and you know it.'

Brad swung his legs off the bed. He explored the bandage neatly wrapped around his head with tentative fingers.

'Don't push yourself, Brad, Doc Grierson said to take care of that shoulder ...'

'It's happened a coupla times before – I first did it roping steers when I was a kid.' Brad paused to look down, relieved to find he was wearing a nightshirt, so he was spared embarrassment in front of Janelle. He reached for his clothes, retrieved his Durham sack, rolled a cigarette and lit it. He drew heavily and let the smoke trickle gently from his nostrils whilst he rasped his bristly cheek thoughtfully with the fingers of his left hand. 'You wanna know somethin'? Those guys laughed when I told them I was a ranger. They made me dance to Colt music. Now that sticks in my craw. When I catch up with them, they're gonna laugh on the other side of their faces. Now leave me while I get dressed.'

He must have spoken with sufficient conviction for Tom and Janelle no longer resisted him. They tactfully withdrew leaving him to get washed, shaved and dressed in his own time – which took long enough, given his right shoulder felt as stiff and hot as a branding iron. But what was more important, it gave him space to think, for his mind was simmering with a lot of questions he wanted answers to.

His bag had been salvaged safely and he was relieved to find his Colt tucked away in his clothing. Cursing his folly, he buckled on his gunbelt and Bowie knife, vowing that he had appeared for the last time in public without them.

He tried a draw, but his shoulder locked solid making him swear with pain. He wasn't ambidextrous; to carry a second weapon on his left hip was pretentious nonsense as far as he was concerned. So, very carefully, he adjusted his holster for a cross-draw from the left. Pain or no pain, he would have to manage it that way.

As he left the bedroom the size of the landing surprised him. A thick pile carpet led away to a large staircase lined with hunting trophies and gilt-framed oil paintings of settlers struggling across primitive western landscapes.

Brad's measured progress from the foot of the

stairs concluded beside a heavy oak door. As he paused, he became aware of a slight movement behind him. With reactions fine tuned to danger, his hand darted instinctively towards his weapon.

He turned to face the solemn faces of two children.

'You must be Uncle Brad,' the girl said.

Brad looked at her and restrained a sharp intake of breath. The freckled face, with the clearly defined cheek-bones framed by the tangle of golden curls made the girl a miniature replica of her mother.

'Pa don't allow no man to wear a gun in the house,' the girl said reproachfully.

Tongue-tied with embarrassment, Brad reholstered his weapon. How the hell did you talk to kids?

Frightened by his uncompromising stare, the boy moved behind his sister.

'Somethin's happened to our ma,' the girl said. 'Maybe you cin tell us? We ain't seen her since yesterday and Pa's bin awful quiet this mornin'.'

'I want my ma.' The little boy screwed both his fists in to his eyes as he began to cry.

Brad's tongue clove to the roof of his mouth. In the presence of this self-assured little girl and the weeping boy, he felt totally inadequate.

The rattle of china saved him. Glancing over his shoulder he saw a door open and a coloured maid appeared carrying a tray.

'Hush now, ma baby, why yo' cryin'?' the maid said. She laid down the tray and bent down to console the boy.

The door opened and Tom appeared. Taking in

the situation he said, 'Oh I see you've met the kids. Come on in, Brad. I guess Hannah and George are too young to understand what's goin' on.'

That's just where you're wrong, thought Brad. They know well enough.

He followed Tom into the room. Janelle was standing by the window, looking out over the open range. She was smoking a cigarette in a long ebony holder.

The maid left the tray on a carved mahogany table.

'Coffee?' Janelle smiled at Brad as the maid retreated.

As he nodded, Brad caught sight of an oil painting on the wall opposite the window. With a start he recognized Beth. It must have been painted a year or so after her marriage, the artist had caught her in full bloom. Her hair was blowing in the wind, her freckled face so full of life it made him choke. She seemed to be smiling directly at him. It was uncanny, as if she were present in the room right now.

The tinkle of cups and saucers broke the tense silence. Tom pulled out his pipe, lit it and began to pace the room. 'This is as bad as being at my command post during the war. If only I knew what was happening, at least I could do something. It's all this uncertainty I can't stand.'

There was the sound of heavy footfalls outside. A tap on the door came as soon as they stopped.

'Come in!' Tom Anderson rapped.

The door opened and a broad-shouldered man lumbered into the room. Dishevelled and unshaven, his range clothes were covered in dust and he was sweating profusely. He carried an envelope in his big hand.

'Well, what is it, Crellin?'

'I got news, Mr Anderson,' the man said urgently. 'One of the boys found this nailed to a corral post close by the water hole.' He shifted uneasily from foot to foot as he spoke.

As Crellin held out the envelope to Tom, Brad saw that it was sealed with wax.

Tom read aloud: "Your wife is safe. If you want her back alive, the price is 50,000 dollars payable in one week from today".'

'So that's it,' he said through clenched teeth. 'It's all about money.'

Brad's brow furrowed as he took the note from his brother-in-law. As he read it, he noticed that the notepaper was good quality and the writing was an educated hand.

Crellin stirred uncomfortably; he was a cow man, obviously out of his depth. 'If I could get my hands on these lousy, rotten bastards!' he burst out. Suddenly he became aware of Janelle's presence and his big hands almost crushed his stetson in embarrassment. 'Why, I'm real sorry, ma'am, I guess I got carried away.'

Brad sympathized. Crellin would spend the rest of the day with his face red as a cockerel's comb at the memory of it.

'You keep this to yourself, you hear?' Tom ordered, his lips compressed as thin as the edge of a Bowie knife.

Crellin nodded. 'Do I keep the boys searchin'?'

Tom hesitated. He turned helplessly towards Brad.

'No use, I reckon,' Brad said. 'They'll have her holed-up someplace by now.'

Crellin looked disappointed.

'I guess you're right,' Tom replied. 'By the way, Art, I didn't get round to introducing you yesterday. This is Brad Saunders, my brother-in-law. He's a ranger. Rides with McNelly's Special Company.'

Art Crellin shook hands warmly with Brad. 'It's good to meet the genuine article. You boys are sure makin' a name for yourselves down Nueces way.' He looked at Brad's bandaged head. 'Too bad about what happened. I bet those kidnappers had no idea who they were tangling with.'

Brad grimaced at the irony of Crellin's remark. Inside he felt as mean and edgy as a tom cat held by the tail, but he kept his cool and said nothing.

'I gotta tell you that me and my boys are riled 'bout this business,' Crellin continued. 'Mrs Anderson is one helluva good woman. If any harm comes to a hair of her head, there's gonna be big trouble.'

Brad warmed to Art Crellin as he returned his handclasp. 'One helluva good woman,' was the highest accolade a cowhand could give a member of the opposite sex.

'You keep your men corralled for now,' he told the Double Circle foreman. 'I don't want no gun-totin' cowboys stirrin' trouble – not until I'm good and ready. You got it?'

As the foreman accepted his authority, Brad felt his confidence rising. The guy was legit, his instinct told him that. At least Tom Anderson didn't have any skin-shedding sidewinders in his

Vacation at San Pedro

employ. What he had to do now was ride into town and start some sleuthin' as soon as possible.

After Crellin had withdrawn, Janelle passed a cup of coffee to Brad. The delicately shaped fingers of the hand that held it were host to a cluster of rings.

Mindful of the social graces, he resisted the temptation to swallow his drink in one gulp. As she patted a loose strand of her ash-blonde coiffure into place, he realized her age was indefinable – she was at that stage of maturity where she could have been anywhere between thirty and fifty. The cut of her dress showed only a hint of cleavage, just enough to promise the swelling maturity of the firm breasts beneath.

'I can't raise this kinda money in cash,' Tom was saying. 'I'll have to either sell or mortgage the ranch. If I do put the place up for sale, no doubt any offer will be well below the market price.'

'Surely it isn't a question of what this place is worth, Tom. Beth's safety comes first,' Janelle said crisply.

With an effort, Brad dragged his eyes away from Janelle. 'Has anyone made an offer, recently?' he followed in.

Tom shook his head. 'Nope. I know of no one who could afford to pay the market price.'

'Someone wants you out, for sure, Tom,' Janelle said.

Tom Anderson spread his arms wide. 'But who?'

Brad's eyes settled on the portrait of Beth. 'Now that's just what I aim to find out.'

'Maybe I should have a word with Mr Kroll,' Janelle suggested. She patted her hair and smiled. 'I'm having lunch with him today.'

Tom Anderson nodded. 'I need to stop by at the bank. I'll drive with you into town. Meantime I'll get Crellin to send one of the boys on ahead to fix a meeting with Frikki this afternoon.'

Leaving Janelle behind in the room, Tom accompanied Brad to the door. As they stepped out onto the stoop, Brad said. 'This election fer mayor – Beth mentioned this guy Frikki Kroll is standin' against you.'

Tom made a wry face. 'Sure. Frikki's a lawyer – and a real smart one, too. He's a bachelor. Since Janelle came to stay with us, he's been very kind to her.' He gave a wry smile. 'Beth's been matchmakin' I guess. Still, I suppose if she's lookin' fer a husband, Janelle could do a lot worse than Frikki Kroll. She's old enough to make her own mind up. Who am I to stand in her way? As far as Frikki and I are concerned, this contest between us for mayor is just friendly rivalry.'

'I guess I'll borrow a hoss from your remuda and ride into town,' Brad said.

'Feel free,' Tom said as he limped after Brad.

With Crellin's help, Brad chose and saddled a strong black stallion from the corral. As he rode in the direction of San Pedro, he pondered Tom Anderson's last words. Friendly rivalry was something new to Brad. Tom Anderson was plainly a very trusting man, for in Brad's experience on the frontier, only the strongest survived – not necessarily the just.

FOUR

Brad rode to the top of a rise, his keen eyes scanning the rugged country rolling away ahead. His horse snorted and backed off uneasily as he caught the scent of the dead animal still lying in the traces of the wrecked buckboard.

'The boss says to shift it once you've taken a look,' offered the young black cowhand Crellin had detailed to accompany Brad. As they approached, the stifling atmosphere rustled with the sound of buzzards' wings.

The ribcage of the dead animal had been picked clean already.

Brad eased the pressure of his stetson on his burning scalp wound as keen eyes scoured the ground for sign. 'Looks like no one else has stopped by since Art Crellin and the boys,' he commented.

'Nope – this trail runs across Mr Anderson's land to the old staging post. Ain't no use fer it otherwise.'

'So the sheriff ain't been,' Brad muttered.

His companion stifled a snigger.

'Guess you don't take no shine to him,' Brad picked him up quickly.

'Guess not.'

Brad rounded on him. 'But he's the law round here, boy. Ain't you got no respect fer the badge?'

The young chap looked defiant. 'The badge means nuthin' – it's the guy who's wearin' it that counts. At least that's the way it is with me.'

Brad left his approval of the boy's sentiment unspoken.

'Can you cut sign, Ranger Saunders?' the cowhand asked.

Brad nodded. 'I'll take me a look-see. Best you ride back and tell Art Crellin to send out a gang to clear this mess up. I'll be through here by the time they arrive.'

The cowhand turned his horse, obviously glad to be on his way, leaving Brad to his own thoughts as he set about to search the area.

The sun was high by the time Brad was satisfied. He had completed his task with his usual meticulous thoroughness and established that there was no sign worth the following. Beth's abductors knew their job – they had covered their trail well.

He took out the makings and rolled a cigarette reflectively. It was no more than he had expected; he had detected a certain professionalism about the one who'd given the orders, *the one with the tattoo of a rattler on the back of his right wrist*. The young guy was greener than High Plains' grass in spring; he could tell that by the sound of his voice and the eager way he had torn open Beth's dress. An outlaw could be made by one thoughtless act, but that didn't guarantee him a job for life. If a youngster didn't learn how to take care of himself pretty fast, he faced an early death.

With a sigh, Brad walked over to his horse, patted him and took a last look at the scene of his humiliation before taking a final drag on his cigarette. He ground the stub carefully into the parched ground.

He shoved his leg into the stirrup and mounted the saddle.

'C'mon hoss,' he muttered. 'Let's go into town and do us a mite of detectin'.'

The arrival of the railway had been the making of towns like San Pedro. Brad noticed a big difference in the place since he'd passed through ten years ago when he'd been stock detecting on the Chisholm Trail with his old buddy Captain Walt Dawson.

The sun rose hot in the sky, there hadn't been any rain for several weeks now and Brad kept his distance, clear of the choking dust kicked up by a wagon team as it lumbered ahead of him, content to take stock of the place.

The trail he was riding led south into the outskirts following the arrow straight lines of the rail track until it reached the elbow of the river where the town began. He rode past several scattered groups of houses before reaching the main thoroughfare, Commercial Street.

There, saloons, thronged with all the riff-raff only the railway could attract, were intermingled with a general store, a saddlery, the office of the *San Pedro Weekly News,* several seedy-looking hotels and a gunsmith's before they eventually gave way to some smarter business premises, the more salubrious looking Glyn Hotel, the Pegg County Offices and then a bank of the same name.

So now he knew he was at the hub of the place. But it wasn't the bank he was after, what he badly wanted to do first was to meet with the sheriff.

A garishly dressed Mexican girl gestured to him suggestively as he rode past the largest saloon he'd seen so far, the Golden Fleece. But Brad hardly saw the honky-tonk's brazen blandishment for he'd just spotted the sheriff's office.

He dismounted and tethered his horse. As he mounted the boardwalk he saw a sign announcing the Town Marshal's office. Peering through the window he saw cobwebs hanging from the ceiling.

'There ain't no marshal, mister,' an old-timer, sitting on a bench outside, volunteered the information querulously. He spat a stream of tobacco juice accurately into the road. 'They reckon this town don't need one.' He concluded his observation with a cackle of cynical laughter.

Brad remounted. From what Crellin's cowhand had told him, he guessed his visit to the sheriff would be a formality.

Ryan was seated, both feet on the desk, his hands clasped over his ample belly, when Brad strode into his office.

When the sheriff didn't react to the door snecking behind him, Brad's cursory glance took in the empty cells and the full gun racks before he stepped forward and tipped the man's stetson back from over his eyes. The dominant smell in the fetid atmosphere was whiskey.

'Wake up!' Brad snapped.

The sheriff stirred. His bloodshot eyes opened. 'What's up? Can't you let a man take his nap in peace?'

Brad sat on the edge of his desk and folded his arms. 'This where you get your inspiration from?' he asked, picking up the half-empty bottle labelled Red Dynamite.

Ryan's eyes narrowed. 'Watch what you're sayin', stranger, I'm the law round here.'

'So how far have you got with your investigation into the abduction of Beth Anderson?'

Ryan swept his feet clear of the desk and sat bolt upright. 'What's it to you?' he demanded.

'The same as it is to everyone round here, 'ceptin' for you, so it seems.'

A small vein began to pulse in Ryan's temple. 'Mister, I don't take kindly to strangers walkin' in here an' tellin' me how to do my job.'

'It ain't a question of how. Way I see it, you ain't doin' it at all.' Brad slid off the desk, placed both hands on it and glared angrily at Ryan. 'I'm Beth's brother. I was with her yesterday when two men jumped us and abducted her.' He touched his head gingerly. 'One of them shot me. I reckon they didn't figure I'd live to tell the tale. But you wouldn't know anything about this for you ain't been near the scene of the crime, have you?'

Ryan rose unsteadily to his feet. 'Now wait a minute! I bin in this law game a long time now. There ain't no earthly reason to go chasin' round bare-assed when there ain't nuthin' to go on. If I did that I'd be all over Pegg County gettin' nowhere.'

Brad pulled away in disgust. He banged the

bottle down on the desk. 'Sheriff, you don't fool me. As from now, the investigation into this case is out of your hands.'

Ryan stared at Brad. 'Just who the hell do you think you are, mister?' he shouted.

'Brad Saunders, McNelly's Special Company, Texas Rangers.' Brad flipped back his vest to reveal the silver star.

Ryan's drink-sodden face turned pale. He gripped the desk for support until his knuckles turned white. 'Ranger you may be, but I know the law. You ain't got no jurisdiction here,' he shouted. 'Not unless it's asked for. Well I'm tellin' yuh, I don't need your help and I ain't askin' for it.'

'Too bad,' Brad retorted. He strode back to the door and paused. 'I don't give a damn what you want Ryan. I'm taking over this case, whether you ask or you don't. So now you can get back to yore bottle.'

'Like hell I will! I'll wire McNelly and have you recalled.'

Brad grinned sourly. 'He won't do that. I'm on vacation.'

Brad remounted and walked the stallion back along Commercial Street. He'd seen washed-up lawmen before but never one as bad as Ryan. The guy was acting like he was in mortal fear of something – or someone.

As he retraced his way along the street, Brad decided to call at the newspaper office.

'Howdy, stranger.' The shirt-sleeved editor pushed up his green cardboard eye-shade as he greeted Brad. 'What can I do fer you?'

'You heard about Mrs Anderson's abduction?'

The editor nodded. 'I'm real sorry 'bout that. She's a real nice lady, but ...' The man shook his head mournfully as he worked an unlit cigar to and fro between his teeth. 'What did she expect when she married a carpetbagger who's got the nerve to stand fer mayor?'

The cigar flew out of his mouth as Brad leaned across the desk, grabbed the man by the collar and jerked him upright.

'That's my sister you're talkin' about.'

'Hold it!'

Brad froze and then slowly relaxed his strangulating grasp on the editor's scrawny neck as he turned to face the shotgun held by the printer who had emerged from the back room.

'Put it down, Pete, fer Gawd's sake,' the editor croaked. 'This guy is Brad Saunders.'

The printer lowered the gun. 'The Texas Ranger? Sorry, mister, but we get all sorts in here.'

'Soon as you said who you were, I figured it,' the editor said. 'We ran an agented piece about that clean-up you did down Espera way.'

'I'm here on vacation,' Brad said. 'But I guess I ain't now.' He eyed the editor with contempt. 'From what you said 'bout my brother-in-law, I guess I can't expect any information from you.'

'Now wait a minute ...'

Brad stalked out of the office and let the door bang shut behind him.

It was late morning now, business was beginning to pick up and as he dismounted and hitched his stallion outside the sign of the Golden Fleece, the high-pitched tinkle of an overstrung joanna belted out the raucous chorus of *Pop Goes the Weasel*.

Thirsty from his dusty ride, Brad nudged through the batwings and headed for the bar.

'Stranger, you look like a man with a throat like the bed of a dry gulch,' the barkeep said. 'Beer?'

Brad nodded and looked around. High over the man's shoulder hung a mirror painted with a picture of a nude girl reclining voluptuously on a sofa.

'Real purty, ain't she, mister?' A woman's voice spoke.

Brad turned to face the woman who had marked his entrance from her vantage point just inside the door. The close-fitting bright red bodice of her dress revealed the deep cleavage of her breasts; the short frilly skirt, trimmed with a green sash, her bare legs disappearing into calf-length boots. She wasn't a day over twenty-five, but her face carried the old-young look of a lifetime's experience. In the distance, the madame hovered like a predator, keeping watch over the outcome of her approach.

'Aintcha gonna buy a girl a drink? My name's Kate – Crazy Kate they call me.' She moved closer in, brushing her uplifted bust against him, the heavy scent of her cheap perfume masking the stale smell of sweat and beer that had hitherto pervaded the atmosphere.

Brad studied the woman for a moment. Every piece of back-street gossip, every scandal that was ever breathed in a town like San Pedro would be known by such a hard-nosed woman as this.

Vacation at San Pedro

If she was disconcerted by his cold appraisal, Crazy Kate showed no sign of it. She waited while Brad pushed a greenback towards the barkeep in exchange for a beer for himself and a glass of cold tea for the woman.

'You wanna dance, play poker, maybe?' She lowered her voice to a husky whisper. When Brad failed to respond, her lips widened in a practised smile, above which her eyes stayed cold and calculating. 'Or maybe iffen you down that drink, we could go someplace where it's nice and quiet.'

Brad nodded almost imperceptibly before he swallowed the beer and followed her up the raked staircase out of the smoke and hubbub of the saloon. A short way along the corridor, the woman pushed open the door to an empty room. The only furnishing was a rumpled bed and a single cane-backed chair, its seat splintered almost beyond repair.

'It's two dollars fer a quickie, mister,' Kate said as she perched on the bed and sank back on to both hands thrusting her breasts forward provocatively.

Brad sat down on the chair. As she made to remove her clothes, he said, 'Hold it!'

The woman stared at him, puzzled. Brad took out his wallet and laid a five-dollar bill on the bed. 'I'm seeking information,' he said.

Kate's eyes gleamed at the size of the greenback, but she wrinkled her nose in disgust. 'Don't tell me you've come a-lookin' fer your long-lost sister.'

Brad winced inwardly at the irony of the remark. He turned back his vest to reveal his badge ...

Levine had entered the town discreetly by a side alley. His horse had lost a shoe, so he left the animal at a farrier not far from the train depot. It was five years since he'd seen the guy and he showed no signs of recognition. Levine grimaced. He must have shoed a lot of horses in five years. He shrugged his shoulders. After his own brief spell of notoriety, why should anyone remember him?

As he entered Commercial Street, the pungent smell of burning hoof horn gave way to that of steak sizzling in the kitchen of a nearby restaurant. The sultry heat of the midday sun hit him as he emerged from the alley. He licked his lips, his mouth felt as parched as sand in the desert. He mopped his brow with his bandanna.

Across the street the sign of the Golden Fleece Saloon beckoned. On the stoop, close by the door, he caught a glimpse of the garish costume of a young Mexican as she took the air.

A sudden feeling that certain possibilities were now open that had been denied to him for five years overwhelmed Levine. Once he had the first payment in his pocket he could start living again. A man-sized steak followed by a willing woman would do for now. There was a spring in his step as he set out to cross the busy street.

'Whoa there, mister, jest you watch yore step!' a hulking teamster shouted down at him from the driving seat of his goods wagon.

Levine hardly noticed as the leading horse brushed past him. His attention was focused on the rider who had just dismounted from his horse and was hitching it to the rail outside the Golden Fleece Saloon.

Levine did a double take and drew a sharp breath.

The man was the brother of Beth Anderson!

He cursed under his breath. He should have stopped to check that Billy Boy's bullet had done its work. You couldn't trust these youngsters these days, they seemed incapable of making a proper job of anything. Just suppose the guy was what he and his sister claimed him to be? The thought nagged at him until it brought a sheen of sweat to his brow. His experience with the law had given him a healthy respect for the consequences of being caught breaking it.

He pondered.

What if he was to follow this man into the Golden Fleece? He'd not set foot in San Pedro since his sentence. There was no way either the women or his quarry would recognize him – and it would give him a chance to check things out.

He sauntered up the steps, nudged through the batwings and stepped inside the saloon, just in time to see his man walking upstairs with one of the women.

'*Buenos Dios, Señor*. My name is Juanita – can I get you a drink?'

Levine hesitated as the woman tugged at his sleeve. Having seen the guy going upstairs with one of these women he ought to have been satisfied, but five years in prison had made him a very suspicious man.

He smiled pleasantly at the woman. She was

young; new to the game for she still had her dark good looks. He wavered. He felt a sudden, almost painful urge. Five years was a long time to go without a woman ...

But he was mature enough to allow reason to hold sway over carnal desire. He swallowed hard. He had no money yet. 'Why Juanita, I'd like to clean up first.'

'*Verdad*? I wish all men were like that.' She pointed a slim finger over his shoulder. 'The men's room is that way.'

Levine's quest brought him out to a dingy passage from which led a flight of stairs. He ignored the men's room and began to mount the stairs. By advancing stealthily, he was able to avoid the loose plank third tread from the top and emerge into a passage off which led several rooms.

A worn piece of coconut matting muffled his progress as he edged from door to door, placing his ear close to each.

His patience was rewarded; every room was empty save one.

What to do?

Levine had reached the age of discretion. To step inside, gun blazing, was too risky. If the guy really was a ranger, he would have to kill him instantly, for the reaction of these men in a tight situation was legendary. Five years of incarceration had done nothing to help his reactions and he knew he couldn't afford to give any advantage away, however slight.

He took a step backwards and pushed open the door into the room adjacent. The stale odour of sweat, tobacco and cheap scent assailed his nostrils. The brass bedstead was stashed hard up against the partition. It was odds on the other rooms had the same layout. He took a step backwards to weigh it up; there would be a matter of only four or five feet between that partition and a similar bed in the room next door.

He unholstered his Colt and knelt gingerly on the bed. The straw filled mattress sagged in the middle, throwing him off balance. A spring creaked as with difficulty he just managed to avoid cracking his skull against the partition.

By wriggling forward he was able to get his ear close to the partition. It was so thin, the conversation of the occupants was clearly audible ...

'You're a Texas Ranger? What the hell do you want with the likes of me?'

'Information. Tell me – how long you worked here, Kate?'

'Waal I started out in San Antonio but I bin around. I've worked for Madame Lafarge for four-five years now.'

'So you reckon you know this town?'

'As well as anyone. Hey, mister, you should see the respectable guys who come creepin' in here after dark. I could name names that would make a few red faces. Them good women they call their wives sure don't keep 'em satisfied.'

'There's someone I need to know about. A lawyer called Frikki Kroll.'

'This got something to do with Tom Anderson's wife disappearin'?'

'You heard 'bout that already?'

'Sure, one of the Double Circle boys rode in earlier on. Went to see the sheriff. Then he called across at the law office before he called in here fer a drink.'

'Listen Kate, I got more than just an interest in this. I was there when it happened. Beth Anderson is my sister ...'

Levine slid back off the bed. So the guy was a genuine Ranger! His lips compressed to a hyphen. If he didn't take this opportunity to get rid of him now, he would live to regret it.

He slipped out his weapon and checked the loads, weighing up exactly where to shoot. He pointed the Colt at the partition and took careful aim. All he needed to do was fan the hammer and make sure he covered the area he had clearly defined in his mind's eye.

His lips curled in a sneer. More than a few eyebrows would be raised when they found Beth Anderson's brother. He could just see the headline in the newspapers: TEXAS RANGER FOUND DEAD IN BED WITH SALOON GIRL.

He licked his lips appreciatively and grinned.

What a helluva way to die!

FIVE

Brad stood up. 'Time ain't on my side, Kate.'

The woman thought for a moment. 'You'll get no help from the sheriff, he's a useless drunken bum. He's in Frikki Kroll's pocket that's fer sure.'

'Kroll?'

Kate nodded. 'He looks a clean-cut, well-set fella, but don't let him fool you. He's just bought this place and raised the rent. It's doubled our prices. Madame Lafarge is hoppin' mad. But he don't care so long as that little Mexican bitch, Juanita, is on heat fer him.'

'Kroll is runnin' fer mayor, agin' Tom Anderson, I'm told?'

'Sure. Shame 'bout Tom Anderson being a Union gen'ral. He's a fine man, but once a carpetbagger, always a carpetbagger, I guess.'

'What chance has he got of bein' elected?'

'I reckon it's touch and go. The war's been over a long time now. Mark you, if he gets elected, a lotta folks in this town will have to mend their ways. Look, mister, time's passin' ...'

Brad stood up and dropped the five-dollar bill on the bed. Before she could pick it up, Brad covered it with the palm of his hand.

'One more thing, Kate,' he said. 'Does this guy Kroll have a tattoo of any kind on his right wrist?'

Kate thought for a moment. 'Nope,' she replied.

Brad withdrew his hand and Kate snatched up the bill. She folded it and as she slipped it between the cleft of her breasts, she stared at him. 'Hey, are you sure you don't want to ...?'

Brad shook his head.

She gave a low whistle. 'Mister, that's the easiest money I earned in a long time.' She looked at him in alarm. 'Say, you won't tell anyone what I said, will you?'

Brad shook his head again.

'I'll let you out the back way.' Kate gave a knowing wink. 'It's the way all the respectable citizens use.'

As she stood up a slight noise came from the room next door.

Kate grinned as she stood up. 'That'll be Juanita. Business is all right for some. These young Mexicans ...'

The blast of a gunshot snatched away her words. It was followed by another – and another ...

Brad lost count as he hit the floor, his hand forking for his weapon down the right side instinctively as bullets whined through the confined space, sparking off the head of the brass bedstead as they ricochetted around the room. The searing pain that racked his right shoulder reminded him he'd slung his holster for a cross draw from the left. By the time he was orientated, the firing had ceased, his ears rang with a silence that sounded shockingly loud and there was no target for him to aim at.

Vacation at San Pedro

He leapt to his feet and reached the door in a bound. Caution made him pause, gun held high as he peered into the corridor. It was deserted, but the door to the next room was ajar. He slid along the wall and kicked the door open but, as he expected, the room was empty; only the whiff of gun smoke betrayed the former presence of the attacker.

Female voices sounded shrill behind him. As he opened the door, he collided with Madame Lafarge. A big, raw-boned, flat-chested woman, soberly dressed in black, she stood out in sharp contrast to the group of gaudily dressed womenfolk who accompanied her.

Suddenly there was a high-pitched scream. 'Kate's bin shot!' shouted one of the women.

Brad shouldered his way past Madame Lafarge. The other women drew back to allow him to re-enter the first room. Kate was lying sprawled on her back on the bed, her legs apart in a grotesque parody of her profession. He took a step forward and bent over her. He needed to look no further, one bullet hole through her temple had been sufficient to kill her, the others through her body only served to add more blood to the ever-widening pool which overflowed from the mattress and dripped on to the floor.

As he turned away, Madame Lafarge appeared in the doorway.

'*Assassin!*' she cried, pointing a bony finger at Brad.

One of the women behind her began to scream hysterically.

As Madame Lafarge recoiled, her place was

taken by the barkeep who pointed the twin barrels of a shotgun at Brad's midriff. 'You'd best have a mighty good explanation fer this, Mister,' he said ominously. 'Kate was a popular gal. There's only gun law in this town – or maybe you fancy a lynching?'

'Now jest hold it,' Brad said, holstering his weapon. He flipped open his vest to reveal his silver star.

The barkeep's face turned pale. He lowered his weapon. 'You a ranger?' Suddenly his eyes narrowed. 'What the hell you doin' in a place like this?'

'Mindin' my own business,' Brad said. 'Which happens to be investigating the disappearance of my sister, Beth Anderson.'

'For that I am sorry, *monsieur,* but what had that to do with Kate?' Madame Lafarge said aggressively.

'Nuthin'. But she told me a few things I needed to know.'

Madame Lafarge drew herself up with aristocratic hauteur. 'You could have asked me, *monsieur.*'

'I could, but I chose not to,' Brad snapped. He jerked his thumb over his shoulder at the body lying on the bed. 'Fer that, I guess you'd better be thankful.'

He took a step forward and pointed at the neat array of five holes in the splintered woodwork of the partition.

With an effort, Madame Lafarge took hold of herself. '*Sacré bleu!* But who has killed her?'

'Those bullets weren't meant fer Kate,' Brad

said. 'They were meant fer me.'

Madame Lafarge followed him as he emerged from the room.

'It ees OK, so you go back to work,' Madame Lafarge snapped at the women. She spread both hands wide in a gesture of resignation as she turned back to Brad. 'What else can I do, *monsieur?* I cannot afford to close.'

Brad nodded grimly. He took a last look at Kate's body, which he had rearranged to a more dignified posture and covered with a spare blanket. An involuntary shiver ran through him. The woman's sudden violent death had shaken him more than he realized.

'Were any of your gals up here?' he asked Madame Lafarge. 'We heard a noise. Kate reckoned it was Juanita.'

Madame Lafarge shook her head. *'Non, monsieur,* she never left the saloon. Kate was the only one who came up here during the last hour.'

Brad gave the woman a penetrating glance. Was she telling the truth?

A sudden draught of air drew his attention to the open window. He strode across to it and looked out across the deserted yard.

Madame Lafarge coughed and said, 'That ees the back way. The way people use when they do not wish to be seen, *vous comprenez?'*

Brad understood perfectly.

He walked back to the door and looked along the passage.

'The stairs at the end lead to the outside door,' Madame Lafarge said.

Brad checked it out. At the foot of the staircase

he noticed there was a door leading into the saloon. The murderer could have made his entry and escaped with ease.

'All the same, I'd like a word with Juanita,' he said.

'As you wish, *monsieur*.'

He followed Madame Lafarge to the top of the staircase.

'Juanita! *Esta usted libre?*' she bellowed down into the half-empty saloon.

'Child, this man, he ees a Texas Ranger,' Madame Lafarge told the girl when she arrived. 'He was asking questions about Mrs Anderson.'

'I know nothing,' the girl said sullenly.

The answer was a mite too pat. Brad knew she was lying.

'*No me gusta,*' he said. 'Kate is dead. It could just as well have been you, Juanita.'

He took a step forward and grabbed the girl by the arm. He took her into the room and jerked back the blanket covering Kate's face, forcing Juanita to look.

The girl recoiled and crossed herself. '*Es horrible!*' she cried.

'I haven't got time to waste,' Brad said harshly. 'Now, tell me all you know.'

Juanita glanced at Madame Lafarge who responded with a curt nod.

'There was a man,' the girl said. 'When I go to him, he asked to go to the men's room first, but he never came back.'

'Think, Juanita,' Brad said slowly. 'What did this guy look like?'

'He was tall and thin. His hair was short. His

Vacation at San Pedro

face was white as flour.'

'You ever seen him before?'

The girl shook her head.

Madame Lafarge spread her hands wide once more. 'My girls, they see so many men ...'

Brad smiled. 'C'mon Juanita, you can do better than this, what else?'

The girl's brow wrinkled. 'The back of one of his hands, it had a mark ... how you call?'

'A tattoo?'

She nodded.

'Think hard, Juanita. What sort of mark was it?'

'A snake perhaps ...'

Brad heaved a sigh of relief. '*Gracias,* Juanita, you've bin a great help.'

'*Un moment, monsieur,* what about Kate?' Madame Lafarge's question detained Brad as he strode towards the stairs.

'See the mortician and send the bill to me,' he said curtly.

SIX

As soon as Brad had left, Sheriff Ryan showed a remarkable turn of speed. In his haste, he knocked over his bottle of whiskey, spilling a pool of amber liquid on to the desk, but he paid no heed.

Jamming his stetson on his head, he emerged from his office and hurried across the street. Although it was barely fifty yards, his heart was pounding and his lungs were pumping for breath as he reached the door at the bottom of the stairs that led to Frikki Kroll's law office.

Miss Rossiter, Frikki Kroll's clerk, looked over her half-moon spectacles in pained surprise as he burst upon her. She laid her pen down on a cut glass inkstand and patted her grey hair with neatly manicured fingers.

'Why sheriff Ryan, what on earth is the matter?'

With an effort, Ryan composed himself. He was unashamedly in love with Miss Rossiter, but even though he had frequently tried to convince her of his undying devotion, she always treated him like a schoolboy.

'I gotta see Mr Kroll,' he spluttered.

Miss Rossiter neatly avoided a gob of spittle

which flew past the lobe of her right ear. 'Oh, I guess Mr Kroll is very busy.'

For once, Sheriff Ryan surprised the cool Miss Rossiter with his tenacity. 'You go tell him I need to speak with him – otherwise I won't be responsible for the consequences,' he rapped.

Miss Rossiter took one more look at Ryan's sweating visage and made her decision.

'Very well,' she said.

Ryan paced up and down in agitation, failing for once to be aroused by the swirl of Miss Rossiter's ankle-length skirt as she went about her errand.

She returned in a few moments, leaving the door ajar.

'Mr Kroll will see you now,' she said.

With a nod of acknowledgement, Ryan composed himself and entered the inner office, closing the door firmly behind him.

Frikki Kroll flicked a speck of cigar ash from the sleeve of his immaculately cut suit and eased his bulk into a more comfortable position in the swivel chair behind the oak desk. As he drew smoothly on his cigar, the warm breeze from the half-open sash window wafted the smoke towards the ceiling.

He looked up as Ryan hurried in, an expression of autocratic surprise on his heavily bearded face. 'Well, Ryan? I hope it's as important as Miss Rossiter tells me, for I'm running late as it is.'

Ryan paused to compose himself.

'Only five minutes ago I just had a fella in my office, wantin' to know why I was doing nothing about Beth Anderson's abduction. Turns out he's her brother. Seems he was with her yesterday when Levine did the snatch.'

Kroll's bushy black eyebrows flicked up a fraction. 'So? What does it matter? I left it to Levine to use his judgement. We never thought it would be possible to find her alone.'

Ryan swallowed hard. 'The guy's a ranger fer Christ's sake! He's one of McNelly's bunch.'

Kroll's eyes narrowed. He leapt to his feet and walked over to the window and stared outside, drumming his fingers on the window ledge, waiting until the rattle of a wagon team, passing by on the street below, abated. Then he whirled round to face the dithering Ryan. 'You sure about this?'

Ryan looked puzzled. 'Of course I am.' He looked anxiously at Kroll's thunderous face. 'Say, what the hell is going on?'

'You're the sheriff, you tell me,' Kroll drawled.

Ryan swallowed with difficulty. 'Seems like the ranger was travelling out to the Double Circle with his sister when it happened.'

'Some ranger! How come he couldn't defend his own sister?'

Ryan shrugged. 'Dunno. Said somethin' about bein' here on vacation. Looks like he got creased in the fracas. But I tell you, he's as mean as a hungry coyote.'

'Hush your mouth! We're miles away from McNelly and his boys.'

The distant hammering of gunshots brought a frown to Kroll's face. 'Sounds like trouble out there again,' he said.

Ryan's face turned white. Beads of sweat formed on his forehead. 'Supposin' that ranger finds out about us?' he croaked.

Vacation at San Pedro

Kroll's face split into a crooked smile. 'Calm down, Ryan.' He drew evenly on his cigar. 'We ain't backing out fer sure, we're in too far. Now you just stay put in your office and do what you're best at – nuthin'.'

'But what are we gonna do about the ranger?' Ryan muttered. 'He told me he's takin' over the investigation. I told him he'd got no jurisdiction without my say-so, but he paid no heed.'

Kroll looked at Ryan with an arrogance bred through his Prussian ancestry. 'Don't you worry none. Just do as I tell you. OK, Levine botched it. So leave him to me – I'm more than a match for any interferin' ranger.'

He walked over to a cabinet, took out a bottle of Lone Star whiskey and poured two generous measures. He passed one to Ryan.

The sheriff downed his at a gulp. 'I ain't done nuthin', just like you said, Mr Kroll,' he burst out. 'But I bin thinkin'. What's Tom Anderson gonna say about that?'

With a sigh, Frikki poured him a refill. 'Why, you've been busy, haven't you? Pegg County is fair bustin' with crime. You're spending every minute jest chasin' your tail ...'

Ryan smacked his lips appreciatively and Kroll refilled his glass.

Kroll watched, his lips curled in contempt as Ryan's next gulp lowered the level in the glass by half.

Ryan's bloodshot eyes narrowed and his cheeks flared pink as the strong liquor took effect. 'That's what I reckon Tom Anderson's gonna say. He don't like the way I do things. If it hadn't been his interfering, Joe would've never served his time the way he had to.'

Kroll scowled. 'That's five years gone. Just glue your backside to your office seat. Fer you, that should be no problem.'

Ryan's temper flared. 'Well, now, I don't care for the way you put that.'

'Have another drink.' The sheriff fell silent as Kroll shoved the bottle towards him.

At that moment there was a knock on the door, Kroll walked over to it and opened it.

'I'm sorry Mr Kroll, but there's another visitor for you,' Miss Rossiter said. 'He wouldn't give his name.'

She stood aside and Levine brushed past her. Kroll closed the door hastily behind him.

'What the hell are you doin' here?' Kroll demanded as Levine picked up a glass and helped himself to the whiskey.

'Jest settling a little unfinished business, as it turns out,' Levine replied.

'Like what? Don't you know the guy who was with Beth Anderson is in town? Ryan's just told me he's a ranger.'

Levine smirked. '*Was*, you mean. I saw him goin' into the Golden Fleece. I decided to finish the job I left to my sidekick the other day.'

'So that was the firin' we heard? You took a helluva risk comin' on here. Anybody see you?' Kroll snapped.

'Even if they did, they didn't recognize me. Beth Anderson didn't. Why, even your clerk didn't just now.'

'What about McNelly?' Ryan whinged.

Vacation at San Pedro

'Shut up about McNelly!' Kroll just managed to prevent himself from shouting. 'He's a dozen counties away from here. We'll have the whole business stitched up before he even hears about it. By the way, where are you holdin' the woman?' he asked Levine.

Levine's eyes narrowed. 'That would be tellin', wouldn't it?' he said.

Kroll shrugged. 'It's OK with me – just as long as you fulfil the bargain.'

'That's no problem,' Levine replied evenly. 'Just as long as you keep your side of it.'

Ryan leaned forward, eyes gleaming. 'Say Mr Kroll, when do I get my cut?'

Kroll corked the bottle. 'When you've earned it,' he said. He slipped his hand inside a pocket in his fancy vest and produced a gold watch. 'I guess it's lunchtime.'

'Say you ain't winin' and dinin' that widow woman from back east, are you?' Ryan's face flared red in alarm. 'She's Tom Anderson's sister, fer Chrissake.'

Kroll's white smile showed a set of gleaming white teeth. 'In the short time we have known each other, Janelle ... er, Mrs Hawk and I have become very good friends. Iffen I drew back now, what might people think?' He walked over to the staghorn rack in the corner, picked up his cane, and put on his hat at a jaunty angle. 'I'm meeting with her at the Glyn Hotel for lunch. It would never do to disappoint a lady, would it?'

Ryan broke into a smile as Kroll escorted him to the door. He shook his head in wonder. 'Jeez, Mr Kroll, that's real smart of you.'

As Kroll opened the door, Miss Rossiter appeared. 'My visitors are just leaving,' he said smoothly.

After Levine and Ryan had gone, Kroll turned on a dazzling smile for his clerk. 'By the way, Elaine, what time have you arranged that meeting for me with Mr Anderson this afternoon?'

'It's at two o'clock, Mr Kroll.'

'And don't forget I shall be out tomorrow afternoon.'

'Very well, Mr Kroll.' Miss Rossiter hesitated. 'Will you be coming to my place for dinner this evening?'

He shook his head. 'Not tonight. I gotta see a client.' He stood behind her and placed both hands lightly on her shoulders. He bent down and kissed the nape of her neck. 'You do understand, Elaine, don't you?' he said.

'I understand,' Miss Rossiter replied, stonily.

Kroll was in confident mood as he picked up his cane and left the office. He strode briskly along the sidewalk towards the Glyn Hotel acknowledging the respectful greetings of his fellow citizens as he went.

The prospect of lunch in the best place in town with the elegant widow from back east contributed vastly to his ebullient mood. It was plain his elegance and charm had impressed her when Tom Anderson had held a dinner party in her honour at the Double Circle on her arrival. He grinned to himself. The irony was that Beth Anderson had made it clear that it was her idea to invite him — no doubt with a piece of matchmaking in mind.

As he passed by the Golden Fleece, he saw a

little knot of people gathered around the entrance. Curious, he walked across the street to take a look. Hank Furman, the mortician, was hovering beside his cart as he arrived.

'Did I hear shootin'?' Kroll asked innocently.

The mortician expectorated neatly over the barrier of the sidewalk. He tilted his hat back and scratched his head reflectively. 'Sure did,' he said.

'Who ...' Kroll's words died on his lips as two men appeared stretchering a corpse. The blanket they had thrown over it did not fully cover Kate's gaudy dress.

Madame Lafarge appeared in the doorway. 'A man – he kill Crazy Kate,' she said sombrely.

'But I thought I heard a lotta shots?' Kroll said.

'Sure,' said Hank. 'But there's only the one corpse. Found it upstairs in one of them rooms. 'Pears some guy tried to turn the partition into a pepperpot.'

Kroll turned away, his face set grim. So Levine had botched it again! The ranger was still on the loose.

Janelle was waiting for him in the foyer as he entered through the swing doors of the Glyn Hotel. When he saw her he could not restrain a sharp intake of breath.

She was dressed in a white long-sleeved blouse set against a black silk skirt trimmed with neat red sash. Her pale complexion was protected from the hot sunshine by a wide-brimmed hat, trimmed with ribbon.

Kroll ran the tip of his tongue appreciatively along his upper lip. 'Janelle, my dear, how nice to see you!' He threw his hat and cane to the coloured doorman as he greeted her.

Conscious that every man in the room was casting envious eyes at him, he bent low to kiss Janelle's hand, the slight click of his heels, Prussian style, adding just that touch of continental courtesy to the proceedings. Out of the corner of his eye he could see the older women in the room whispering and nodding their approval.

'Did you ride in with Tom?' he enquired as he offered Janelle his arm ready to escort her into the dining-room.

She nodded. 'He's stopped by at the bank.'

'Ah, to try to raise the money for the ransom, I assume.'

'Yes, he felt he ought to make some preliminary enquiries.' Janelle sighed and brushed a tear from her eyes as she sat down. 'I'm worried, Frikki. What's gonna happen to Beth? If anything bad happens it will destroy Tom fer sure. There's no way he can raise that kind of money.'

Kroll paused to order a bottle of claret from the hovering waiter before he slid a comforting hand across the table to enclose Janelle's. 'Don't worry, my dear,' he said. 'Money is what these people are after. They don't want to harm Beth, I'm sure. Everything will turn out just fine in the end, you'll see.'

He sat back in his seat and nodded pleasantly to the neighbouring diners. As he sipped a taster from the glass of wine the waiter brought on a silver salver he found that the prospect of complete victory was enough to intoxicate him. But it behoved him to be careful of the ranger ...

SEVEN

Brad was waiting on the sidewalk outside Kroll's office when Tom Anderson's buggy drew up.

As he stepped forward to help Janelle down, Brad took a sharp intake of breath. The effect of her appearance on the casual loungers and other passers-by on the sidewalk was equally as stunning.

As they entered the main office, Miss Rossiter came forward to meet them. As soon as she saw Tom Anderson she burst out of her mask of cool decorum. 'Tom, I'm so sorry about what's happened,' she said.

Tom rested his weight on his stick and patted her hand. 'You've been a good friend to her, Elaine,' he said.

The inner door opened and Kroll appeared.

'Tom, what can I say?' he said.

As the two men shook hands, Brad saw that Kroll couldn't keep his eyes off Janelle.

They walked into Frikki's office and sat down in the circle of chairs Miss Rossiter had already arranged for them around her employer's desk. She sat apart in one corner, a sombre contrast to the elegant Janelle in her half-moon spectacles and neat grey dress. She licked her pencil and smoothed down the pages of her stenographer's pad resting in her lap as Kroll opened the proceedings.

'Tom, I see from the note you sent me this morning that a ransom of fifty thousand dollars has been demanded?'

Tom nodded and handed over the notice.

Kroll pursed his lips in a silent whistle. 'That's a lot of money.' He turned to Brad. 'It would seem that we are fortunate to have the services of a Texas Ranger?'

Brad nodded. 'Sure. I've taken over the investigation. I talked with Sheriff Ryan this morning and I don't figure he's up to it.'

'What's the legal position, Frikki?' Tom asked. 'You know I'm an upholder of the law.'

Kroll frowned. 'Sheriff Ryan is within his rights to forbid outside interference unless he asks for it.'

'But we all know Ryan is nothing but an incompetent drunkard!' Tom exploded. 'The investigation will get nowhere if it's left to him.'

Kroll pursed his lips thoughtfully. 'I agree. Look I'll be frank, Tom, you and I are both standin' for mayor. But I can't bring myself to take the slightest advantage of you in this unfortunate situation. Ryan's days as sheriff of Pegg County are numbered and in view of the severity of this matter, I suggest that we allow Ranger Saunders to proceed as he thinks fit. I'm sure I can square the other town councillors on this one.'

Tom tapped his stick impatiently. 'Very well. It will look better if it comes from you.' He turned to

Vacation at San Pedro

Brad. 'Now I understand there's been a recent development?'

Brad shrugged, painfully aware that the incident at the Golden Fleece did him no credit. 'Some guy took a shot at me and killed a woman I was questioning,' he said, off-handedly.

'Any idea who?' Kroll's bland expression gave nothing away.

Brad shook his head. 'We rangers make lots of enemies. Could be some guy who recognized me from way back and took his chance.'

'Better be careful what kinda place you frequent in future, Brad,' Tom said, reproachfully.

Brad, who was sitting opposite Janelle, avoided the amused look in her big round eyes.

'Well, now,' said Kroll, briskly. 'It don't look like Ranger Saunders has got much to go on, so, speakin' as your lawyer, Tom, I guess we've gotta prepare for all eventualities. The priority is to get your wife back and you have to face the possibility that at the end of the day you might have to pay.'

Tom nodded dolefully, 'I reckon that, too,' he said. 'That's why I requested this urgent meeting with you. I can't let Beth go without doin' something. If that means payin' the ransom then so be it.'

The expression on his face as he spoke reminded Brad of a colonel he'd once seen whose entire regiment had been cut to pieces.

'That's why you stopped by at the bank on the way here, I take it?' Kroll pressed him gently.

'Sure,' Tom said. 'Look, I'll level with you. There ain't no way I can raise the money. Best I can do is five thousand. The bank will loan the full amount, but they want the ranch as collateral.'

'And no doubt they'll charge the goin' rate?'

Tom nodded. 'Two per cent per month.'

'Why, that's usury!' Janelle exclaimed. 'Is there no chance of an outright buyer for the ranch?'

Tom and Frikki Kroll shook their heads in unison.

'Not a chance,' Tom said. 'The cattle business is in recession, there ain't no buyers around.'

Kroll nodded agreement. He leaned forward and pushed a box of cigars towards Brad and Tom. Tom took one absent-mindedly. Brad refused.

'I can raise the money,' Janelle said quietly. 'If I instruct my bank to sell some stock and bonds I can raise the entire amount.'

The atmosphere in the office changed abruptly.

'Janelle, I can't ask you to lend me money,' Tom said. 'Why, it's gonna take me years to repay the bank.'

'I'm family, Tom, I'd like to help,' Janelle's lips curved into a soft smile.

'The only guarantee I can offer is a share in the ranch,' Tom said.

'I'll settle for that,' Janelle said quietly.

'You can't do it!' Tom gasped. 'I can't possibly take your money.'

Kroll cleared his throat. 'Think about it, Tom. I know I'm not doin' the bank a favour, but as your lawyer, I gotta recommend you seriously consider your sister's most unselfish offer.'

Tom shook his head. 'I need time to think about this.'

'I'll get a valuation and draw up the necessary documents just in case,' Kroll said.

Brad glanced at him, but there was no note of

triumph in the man's voice; to all intents he was a lawyer, doing a competent job.

'Look, I'll wire my bank in New York,' Janelle said. 'These things take time to arrange. Don't wait too long, Tom, before you make your mind up.'

Kroll picked up the note and scanned it again. 'This ain't uneducated scrawl,' he announced. 'I'm sure, when the time comes, the people responsible for this will be more than willing to negotiate an extension.'

'I only hope you're right,' Tom said. 'But I don't like to take your money, Janelle – not for a reason like this.'

'I understand,' she replied softly. 'This has all come as a big shock. But I want to help. I surely do.'

Kroll permitted himself a slight smile. 'In the meantime let's hope Ranger Saunders can come up with somethin'.' He stood up and held out his hand to Tom. 'I'm real sorry it's come to this. Don't hesitate to let me know as soon as you come to a decision.'

He turned to Brad and shook hands with him warmly. 'Good luck with your investigation, Ranger Saunders.'

'You ridin' back with us, Brad?' Tom asked.

Brad shook his head. 'Don't you pay no mind 'bout me,' he said. 'I got things to do.'

Tom nodded. Kroll escorted Janelle across to the waiting carriage in front of a group of gawping loungers.

Once Brad had seen them off, he left Kroll's office and went across to the Golden Fleece.

Brad's entry into the saloon was noted, but none of the women approached him. The barkeep pushed a beer across to him and held up his hand in refusal when he offered payment.

Brad rolled a smoke and pondered. He was getting no place fast on this one. A mind full of suspicions was one thing, but what he needed was hard evidence.

Somehow he had to trace the man who had killed Crazy Kate. He was convinced there was a link between this attempt on his life and Beth's abduction. One of the two guys responsible must have been hanging around town and seen his own arrival. Was Beth being held somewhere in town? He dismissed that as too risky. There must be plenty of suitable hiding places within twenty miles of the town. And this man Levine had an accomplice – a much younger man, who had seemed far less in control of himself.

He took a deep draw on his cigarette. What he'd seen and heard back in Kroll's office troubled him. It all sounded so plausible. Was Tom Anderson being cruelly duped? If so, what evidence had he got to prove it?

As he gulped his beer, he became aware of Juanita standing alongside him.

'Señor, there is this note for you,' she said softly.

Brad downed his glass and took the envelope off her. He tore it open.

It read: *Meet me at the bridge over Alexander's Creek at 8 p.m.*

There was no signature.

As Juanita made to leave, Brad grabbed her arm. 'Who brought this?' he asked her.

Juanita shrugged. 'Questions! Always you ask questions! Why you not leave Juanita alone?'

'You ain't leavin' 'till I get an answer,' Brad held out.

Juanita saw the stubborn glint in his eyes and relented. 'A little boy, he bring it. He no say from who. Would he tell me if I ask? Now let me go!'

As the girl withdrew, Brad leaned back and scratched his head. What was he to make of this? Was it some kind of trap?

He wrinkled his nose reflectively. Should he go? A grim smile crept across his face as he realized he had no choice, for this slender lead was all he had to go on.

EIGHT

Kroll finished tidying his desk and took a last look around his office before he bolted and locked the door. He glanced at his watch. It was half past six. Elaine Rossiter had left half an hour earlier. There was time enough to slip across to the Golden Fleece before he headed for his own home on the outskirts of town.

He emerged into the street and set off purposefully in the direction of the saloon. A few steps along the boardwalk brought him level with the alley that ran down the side of the Golden Fleece. He eyed the sign with a proprietary air. The saloon lived up to the irony of its name. Boom times lay ahead, he could sense it. And Kroll, with his ever-increasing sense of rapacity, intended to be first among the pickings.

Juanita was lingering at the foot of the stairs inside the back entrance when he arrived. Her face brightened when she saw him. *'Buenos tardes, señor,'* she said. 'I am so glad you come.' But he could tell by the look in her eyes that the girl was unhappy.

Kroll said nothing, but followed her up the stairs. At the top they turned away from the line of rooms along the upper corridor to enter a bedroom. In contrast to the spartan facilities offered to the *hoi polloi,* this room was furnished with a large canopied bed, a thick-pile carpet and – a personal addition since Kroll had become the owner – full-length gilt mirrors hanging on each wall.

Once inside and with the door closed, he was in a different world from the noise and sweat of the saloon below. Flower scents rose from Juanita's sleek black hair as she clung to his arm.

'You like Juanita – *si?*' Her lips nuzzled his ear provocatively as she spoke.

Her white arms gleamed in the lamplight as she twined them round Kroll's neck. He felt himself grow weak as her fingers teased through his hair. Her firm young breasts pressed against him as she whispered, 'Frikki, when will you take me away from here?'

Kroll took her lips savagely.

'I do not like it here,' the girl said during a pause. 'Kate is killed today.' She shuddered. 'Tomorrow it is me – *no se.*'

Kroll placed his hands on her hips possessively. 'Don't worry, honey. Has anyone any idea who did it?'

Juanita shook her head. 'There was a ranger here – he ask also the same question. I tell him about the man I think has shot Kate.'

'You got a look at him? Can you tell me what he looked like?'

He listened as Juanita described Levine.

'But there is something else,' Juanita said. Her eyes widened in a sly smile. 'This ranger, he get message from the *señorita* who works for you.'

Kroll drew back and frowned. 'Miss Rossiter?'

'*Si*. I ask the boy who bring it – I give heem money and he tells me everything. He say the ranger and she meet at your office this afternoon.' Juanita snapped her fingers and whirled round. 'So – it ees so simple – *si?*'

Kroll listened to the girl with mounting impatience. Why did Elaine Rossiter want to see the ranger? Had she picked up something that made her suspicious over his involvement in Beth Anderson's abduction? Suddenly it clicked. Of course – she must have recognized Levine!

His brain began to function with the urgency of a mill-race. If the ranger was on to Levine, it was time he made his move. One thing was certain: he had to find out what Elaine Rossiter was up to as soon as possible.

He glanced at his fob watch. 'I guess I gotta go,' he told Juanita.

The girl's face flashed in anger. 'But you have not ...'

'Tomorrow, maybe,' Kroll snapped. 'Meantime I've just remembered there's something urgent I gotta attend to.'

The girl came in close. 'But you do not tell me when you take me away from here?' she whispered.

'Not now, Juanita,' Kroll said as he headed for the door.

The girl pouted and clung to him. 'You promised!'

Kroll disentangled himself and pushed her away. 'I know I did, honey, but not right now.'

Vacation at San Pedro

As he headed for the door Juanita intercepted him and barred his way.

'So, you go to her now, eh?' she spat.

Kroll was taken aback by the ferocity in her expression. 'What are you talkin' about, Juanita?'

'Today you take lunch with a woman. At the smart hotel. With the one who stay at the Double Circle.'

Kroll relaxed and smiled. 'Oh, you mean Mrs Hawk? Look you don't understand, Juanita. She's what we lawyers call a client. We were discussin' business. There ain't nuthin' between me and her.'

He kissed Juanita again. 'I gotta go now,' he told her.

She watched him, hands on hips, a disbelieving look on her face as he took the stairs two at a time and disappeared through the door into the yard at the back.

Kroll hurried across to his office. In the drawer lay the only small weapon he possessed – a small calibre derringer. He was no gunman but he loaded it and pushed it into his vest pocket. Sooner or later he figured he might have need of it. That done, he locked the office and strode across to the livery barn.

'You're early tonight, Mr Kroll,' the old-timer in charge for the evening commented as Kroll walked in.

Kroll didn't answer. 'Get my hoss, quick,' he snapped.

He paced up and down impatiently while the old-timer fetched his tack and saddled and bridled his horse. When the animal was ready, without a word of thanks, he mounted up and rode out of town.

His objective was Elaine Rossiter's cabin, which lay in a secluded glade in an oak forest about a mile from the bridge across Alexander's Creek, some three miles south east of the town.

As he drew closer, Kroll slowed his pace, keeping a sharp watch on the trail ahead. He crossed the bridge and then turned off to follow the trail that wound uphill beside the creek until the cabin came into sight.

He dismounted well short of the cabin, tethered his horse and went forward on foot to investigate. As he drew closer, the door opened and Elaine Rossiter emerged. Dressed in levis, a check shirt and vest, she looked for all the world like a young cowhand as she swung easily astride the saddle of her horse.

Kroll drew back behind the trunk of an oak as she trotted the animal away from the cabin and out on to the trail. She was on her own, but it would soon be dusk and the moon was full. Where the hell was she going at this time of night?

He waited until she had moved away along the trail before he checked out the cabin. It was empty. Then he retrieved his horse and rode after her.

Kroll knew his limitations. He knew nothing of tracking, but as long as he used his common sense and his clerk kept to the clearly-defined trail, following her was no problem.

Taking care not to get too close, he rode steadily after her. As he reached the point where the trail from the cabin joined with the main trail he had a

Vacation at San Pedro

clear view of the bridge. Elaine Rossiter had dismounted and was talking with a man.

Kroll eased his horse off the trail and into the woods. A little way ahead he saw a knoll which he made sure overlooked the bridge. He dismounted and crept stealthily forward until he was able to look down on the couple who were talking on the trail below him. He needed only a few seconds to confirm his suspicions.

His clerk was having a secret meeting with the ranger!

NINE

Brad checked out his route and rode out of San Pedro, following the trail south-east as it wound through rugged thickly forested terrain. He took care to arrive at the bridge across Alexander's Creek a good half-hour before the appointed time.

He dismounted and inspected the bridge. A wooden structure, crudely built from the indigenous oaks, it rested on trestles spanning the creek some fifty feet above the water as it foamed past the jagged rocks jutting up from the bed.

He had met nobody on the journey and he intended to complete his reconnaissance of this lonely place well before dusk, for he was taking no chances. By the appointed time, he was familiar with every inch of the terrain and had found a spot in the forest from which to observe anyone approaching the bridge from either end.

The appointed time arrived and passed. He was just becoming restless when the drumming of hooves caught his attention.

Was this the man who wanted to see him?

In the gathering gloom, he was compelled to wait until the rider came closer. He slowed to a canter and then to a walk, finally bringing the horse to a halt.

Brad took a deep breath. The rider had dismounted only a few yards away from him. He was of slight, almost boyish build, that much he could see.

Brad drew his Colt and stepped forward. 'Hold it right there, mister,' he said crisply.

'I see you don't take any chances, Mr Saunders.'

Brad lowered his weapon involuntarily. The precise, clipped tone of Miss Rossiter's voice took him completely by surprise.

She tipped back her stetson to reveal her face and gave a low musical laugh. 'I guess you've gotten a shock from when you last saw me.'

'You could say that,' Brad agreed, holstering his gun.

'When I ain't working at the office, I like nothing better than to ride the range,' she said. 'Beth is the same. Come the weekend we dress like cowpokes and have ourselves a ball.'

That figured. That was Beth through and through. Brad warmed to Miss Rossiter. 'So you and Beth are friends?'

She nodded. 'Sure. I'm real concerned about what's happened to her.'

Brad did not reply.

He was listening to a slight rustling noise, high on the knoll above. It might have been the evening breeze sighing in the trees but Brad wasn't prepared to take any chances.

Without a word he leapt forward and bore Elaine Rossiter to the ground with a jolt that sent a shaft of pain knifing through his shoulder.

'Keep down!' he urged.

He drew his gun again and waited, tense and expectant, but nothing happened.

'Stay right here!' he snapped.

Suddenly he jack-knifed to a crouching position and charged, head down, gun blazing up a short slope towards the knoll outlined against the now starlit sky.

But when he reached the summit there was nothing to be seen.

He reloaded and returned to the woman and helped her to her feet.

'Sorry, Miss Rossiter, false alarm. I guess I'm feelin' kinda spooky.'

She dusted her pants. 'You sure do give a gal a warm reception,' she said crossly. 'But I guess you got every right to be wary. Look, Mr Saunders, what I gotta say is gonna take time. I don't feel safe out here now. Ride back with me to my place. It ain't far. I'll get some food into you and then we can talk.'

Brad felt his cheeks on fire with embarrassment. 'Well, now, Miss Rossiter ...'

'Gosh almighty, boy, what's bitin' you? I'm nigh old enough to be your mother. Now git on your horse and let's get outa here; this place gives me the creeps.'

Brad didn't answer.

The woman shivered. 'You comin' or not?' she pressed him.

For answer, he mounted his horse and followed her along the now moonlit trail across the bridge. She led the way along the side trail until she reached the cabin.

'Pa built this place,' she told him. 'When he first

came out west his ambition was to own a farm. A riding accident put paid to that.'

They dismounted and led their animals past a hen coop and into a barn. Once they had groomed the horses and settled them with feed and water, Miss Rossiter led the way into the cabin.

The door had no lock. It swung open on rawhide hinges to reveal a single room with a stone chimney and a hearth at one end. Miss Rossiter walked over to the log fire and stirred it with a poker. The crane squeaked as she swung the heavy cast-iron stewpot over the flames.

'Take a seat,' she said, indicating a crudely made rocking chair. She lit an oil lamp and then busied herself laying out two places with wooden bowls and spoons.

When she had finished she rigged a curtain. A few minutes later, Brad blinked in amazement. She emerged from behind it, having changed out of her range clothes into a pale blue silk dress. In one day she had completed a metamorphosis from a bespectacled stenographer to cowgirl and now into a very attractive woman.

'I cain't entertain a man lookin' like one,' she said with a smile. 'How do I look?'

'Pretty good,' Brad admitted.

She laughed and gave him a playful dig in the ribs. 'What you mean is not bad for a woman risin' fifty.'

'Miss Rossiter, I take it you wanna talk about Beth's disappearance,' Brad said tactfully as she ladled a generous helping of beef stew into the bowls.

She nodded. 'Set yourself right here.' She drew

up a chair to the puncheon table and sat opposite him. 'Let's eat first, we'll talk over coffee afterwards.'

It was the best idea Brad had heard yet. Miss Rossiter's appetite bettered his and only the clatter of their cutlery and crackling of the fire broke the stillness in the cabin. Afterwards, sat back in the rocking chair with a mug of coffee, Brad waited until Miss Rossiter joined him.

'I expect you're wonderin' why I ain't married,' she said.

Folks had a strange way of getting round to what they wanted to say. Brad had long since learned to be patient. But it was a relevant question. Most decent women who looked half as attractive as Elaine Rossiter were snapped up as soon as they appeared on the frontier. 'It has kinda crossed my mind,' he admitted.

'It all happened at once,' Miss Rossiter said. She sipped her coffee reflectively. '55 was a bad year. Ma died, Pa had his accident and Sam, the guy I was gonna marry, was killed in a hold-up at the bank. He worked there as chief clerk.'

'You lived here then?' Brad said as he rolled and lit a cigarette.

Miss Rossiter nodded. 'I helped build this place. After the accident, Pa had to give up the idea of raising cattle. But he was no quitter, he rallied and started a general store in town. I helped him with the books and ordering stock. We did OK, built the place up until one day a fire burned our warehouse to the ground.'

'Weren't you insured?' Brad asked.

She nodded. 'Of course. But when we came to

claim we found the insurance company back east had gone bankrupt. All our money was tied up in that stock. We were ruined. The shock did for Pa, his heart gave out.'

'So that left you with nothin'?'

Miss Rossiter paused as her face grew sombre with memories.

'Frikki Kroll was our lawyer. He knew I was destitute, so he offered me a job. He was sorry for me, I guess.'

'How long have you worked for him?'

'Just over five years.'

'You oughta know the way he works then.'

Miss Rossiter looked at him sharply. 'You're no fool, Mr Saunders. I watched you in that meeting this afternoon. You were weighing everyone up – including me. You suspect that my boss is involved in this business, don't you?'

Brad flung his stub into the dying embers of the fire. 'Miss Rossiter, iffen you've got somethin' to tell me, then you'd better do it right now.'

She frowned. 'I wouldn't do this, if it wasn't for Beth. But this morning Frikki ... Mr Kroll, had a meeting with the sheriff and another man.'

Brad sat upright. 'Was this 'bout noon?'

She nodded. 'I never seen Ryan move so fast. He came in first demanding to see Mr Kroll – and he sure looked a worried man.'

'He'd a right to be,' Brad muttered. 'Any idea as to what they spoke about?'

Miss Rossiter coughed discreetly. 'Any time Mr Kroll has business he doesn't tell me about, it makes me kinda curious. If I pretend to look at the files in the cabinet by the wall I can just pick up the gist of any conversation that's goin' on in his office.'

Brad leaned forward. 'And ...?'

'Ryan was scared witless by your visit. He told Kroll you were a Ranger.'

'How did Kroll react?'

'He knew nothing about it – until Joe Levine arrived.'

'This guy Levine. D'you know anything about him?'

'Levine was the first guy Kroll defended when I started work with him just over five years back. He was a gambler – the real thing, not a two-bit hustler. One Saturday night, one of Tom Anderson's cowhands made the mistake of thinking he could clean him out. He ended up seven hundred dollars in debt. When he couldn't pay, Levine back-shot him in cold blood – the bullet lodged near the man's spine and left him crippled for life. Tom Anderson was furious – he had Levine brought to justice and Levine got five years with hard labour.'

'Enough to give him reason for revenge,' Brad said. 'Tell me, did Levine have a tattoo on his right wrist?'

Miss Rossiter nodded. 'Sure. That's how I recognized him. The design is a striking rattler.'

She rose and stirred the embers with a poker. Then she turned back to face Brad. 'Kroll is in this up to his neck. So is Ryan – Kroll told him to stay in his office and do nothing. But Levine is crafty – he wouldn't tell Kroll where he's holdin' Beth. I reckon Kroll could be in for a nasty shock if he ain't careful.'

Brad shot a penetrating glance at the woman.

'Miss Rossiter, why are you tellin' me this? Surely loyalty to your boss must carry some weight with you?'

'I'm telling you because I've put two and two together and I didn't like what I came up with. Kroll and Tom Anderson may appear to be on good terms – after all, Kroll is Tom's lawyer. But, believe me, they are deadly rivals for mayor. The stakes are high. It's Kroll's big chance to gain complete control of the town. He's just bought the Golden Fleece. Now if Kroll wants to fall out with Tom Anderson, that's one thing, abducting his wife is another and I fer one ain't standin' fer it.'

Brad drummed his fingers on the arm of his chair. Miss Rossiter had just given him his first hard information so far. But why was she doing this? Was her friendship with Beth sufficient motive for her to betray her boss? Had she been followed to their meeting at the bridge across Alexander's Creek?

'What you gonna do now?'

Brad would not be drawn. He had long since learned not to be a fount of information.

'I can tell you that Mr Kroll is going out of town to a meeting tomorrow afternoon,' Mis Rossiter said. 'It's another of his secrets. He hasn't told me who it's with or where it is. Don't worry, I'll find out though.'

Brad shook his head. 'Don't push too hard. You just go into work as usual. In view of what you've just told me, I'll keep Kroll's movements under surveillance from now on.'

He rose from his chair. 'Well, now, thanks fer your hospitality, Miss Rossiter …'

She looked at him in surprise. 'Hey now, just where do you think you're goin'?'

'Maybe I'll ride back into San Pedro, check into a hotel fer the night.'

'There's no need to do that.' She looked troubled for a moment. 'Look it's gettin' late. That business earlier this evening has kinda scared me. I'd appreciate it if you'd stay.'

Brad coloured slightly. 'Well, now, Miss Rossiter ...'

She laughed. 'Fer pity's sake, call me Elaine. You're safe here with me. I can soon rig a curtain at bedtime. Mind you there's always the barn outside if you feel your honour's at stake.'

He grinned sheepishly. 'I'm sorry, Miss Rossiter, I guess I meant no offence.'

She grinned and slid easily into a broad Texas drawl. 'Iffen I was twenty years younger, I guess I'd be sparkin' fer you. But I guess you'll just have to make do with a hand at cards and a durned good breakfast.'

TEN

Beth watched Billy Boy's behaviour as he prowled the interior of the barn, bursting with all the frustration of a bored dog.

'Where the hell is Joe?' he exploded at last. 'We're supposed to be pardners, how come I get all the lousy jobs?'

Beth didn't answer him. How did he think she felt? She was sitting in a dark corner on a pile of straw, knee haltered with a thong of rawhide. Her hands were free and she had been able to effect a running repair to hold her dress decently. In the odd moment, she had tried to tamper with the bonds which bound her feet, but she had given up in disgust. It would take a razor-sharp knife to release her, but even if she had one, where could she go? Even if she could secure the horse while her captor was asleep, she would soon be lost in the forest.

All the same, Billy's question worried her. What would happen if his companion didn't return? The thought of being left completely at the mercy of this half-witted boy made her blood run cold. Confident though she was that she had won moral supremacy over him, at all costs she must not risk attracting his unwelcome attention.

The night had been long, the heat of the day oppressive. Used to having every minute occupied, time was dragging like a cow coming out of a mud-hole. She tried to speed its passage by thinking of Tom and the kids. She was desperately worried about Brad. She took refuge in the belief that he was tough and durable, he wouldn't have survived the war if he hadn't been.

She began to feel the first twinge of despair. Times were bad, how would Tom raise cash for the ransom except by going cap in hand to the bank?

Janelle was a wealthy woman ... what did she make of Janelle? She had only met her once at the wedding. Tom's sister was a different breed, she was from the north. Alongside the elegant Janelle, she felt like a dray horse next to a thoroughbred mare.

It seemed an eternity before the drumming of hooves heralded the absent man's arrival.

'Where the hell have you bin?' Billy Boy demanded when Levine appeared in the doorway.

From her position in deep shadow, Beth recoiled as she saw the triumphant expression on the older man's face.

'I'll tell you. I finally did fer the ranger, that's what I did.'

Beth felt a wave of nausea pass through her as Levine strode over to where she was sitting and stood over her, his hands resting on his hips.

'You hear that, Mrs Anderson?' he taunted. 'That brother of yours is dead.'

'I don't believe it ...' Beth whispered brokenly.

'He really was a ranger, too.'

Vacation at San Pedro

'Hey, Joe, you killed a ranger? Say, how was it? Did you outdraw him?' Billy Boy danced and fawned round Joe as he spoke, his attitude changing abruptly from childish insolence to hero-worship.

Levine shook his head. 'Listen, Billy Boy, you don't give a Ranger time to draw.' He sniggered. 'Why, you don't even let him know who's shootin' at him.'

'You mean you back-shot him?'

'In a manner of speaking. While he was having fun with a honky-tonk at the Golden Fleece.'

'That's a lie!' Beth said heatedly.

'So? You think your brother wasn't that kinda guy? Well, I guess it don't matter now, I filled him with more holes than a colander.' Levine came closer to Beth as he spoke. 'Matter of fact my own errand at the Golden Fleece got kinda interrupted ...'

As Levine's eyes fell on Beth she shrank back against the wall.

Levine turned to Billy Boy. 'Say, brew some java, will ya? I'm parched.'

He waited while Billy Boy had left before he came over to Beth.

As he placed his hands on her shoulders, Billy Boy shoved his head back through the door. 'Say, Joe, did you get paid?'

Levine let go of Beth and rounded on Billy Boy. 'Like I said, I went into town to get supplies,' he said harshly.

Billy Boy held out his hand. 'Aw c'mon, Joe. Don't gimme hogwash. I want my cut.'

Levine's face turned thunderous. 'Well now

Billy Boy, just what do you mean by that?'

'I mean like we're pardners. Like you said back in Austin. You said if I rode with you we'd split everything.'

'Did I? Waal, I guess I don't remember sayin' that.'

'You did!' Billy Boy's voice rose to a childish pitch.

Joe held up his hands in a placatory gesture. 'Sure, sure, Billy Boy, I'll square with yuh when the deal's through. Gimme a few more days and you'll be a rich man.'

'I want it now,' Billy said ominously.

'Well you ain't gettin' any, 'cos as a matter of fact I ain't got none.'

'You're jokin'.'

'Nope.'

'You're a liar, Joe. I don't believe you killed that guy. You just bin in town a-whorin'.'

'Suit yoreself.'

Beth gasped as Levine laughed and turned his back contemptuously on Billy Boy. He grabbed hold of Beth and took her lips savagely.

'You ain't havin' her!'

With a snarl like a cougar, Billy Boy leapt on to Levine's back and bore him down onto the ground. He was more heavily built than his opponent, but the older man was in hard physical condition. In a lithe movement, Levine wriggled clear and found his feet faster than his stockily built assailant.

Beth winced as Levine's fist jabbed systematically and accurately on to Billy Boy's nose, spattering blood over her as well as the two men. But Billy Boy had been raised tough; as Levine bored in with both fists, he lashed out with one foot, hitting Levine on the shin with a crack like a blunt axe bouncing off hard wood.

Levine cursed in agony, hopping round until he came to rest against the wall, gasping for breath. Billy Boy stood back and laughed maniacally and then, pawing the blood from his face, charged forward ...

The two men clashed and fell in a heap by the door, rolling over and over. With cunning born by years of experience, the older man saw just a half-chance and brought his knee up hard into Billy Boy's groin.

Billy Boy's cry of anguish made Beth's blood run cold. He doubled over retching in agony, his hands clutching his groin. She watched, fascinated, as Levine uncoiled from the floor and sensing his opponent's weakness, attacked, both fists smashing into Billy Boy's already puffed and swollen face.

Billy Boy was fighting blind now, blood streaming down his cheeks from a cut high on his forehead and another on his cheekbone. His counterpunches became weaker as Joe circled him, concentrating his attack on his face, mercilessly punching it to a bloody, unrecognizable mess.

Finally as Levine stood back to summon his strength, Billy Boy lay back against the wall, both arms hanging slackly by his sides, his breath coming in whooping gasps. Suddenly he pitched forward towards Joe.

'No!' Beth screamed involuntarily.

But nothing could stop Levine now. He smashed

his fist deep into Billy Boy's stomach, doubling him over to receive the full force of his knee into his already pulped face, smashing him back against the wall.

There was silence for a moment, before a scraping noise as Billy Boy's heavy torso slid slowly to the ground.

Levine turned slowly towards Beth. His breath came in sharp gasps. She drew back, aware now that not even the half-witted Billy Boy stood between her and the final humiliation.

Suddenly Levine stopped and slid his hand around his chest, wincing as he did so. 'Goddammit, feels like a busted rib,' he said hoarsely.

Before Beth could reply, he toppled forward and lay still.

Beth stared at the two men, too stunned to move. Suddenly it dawned on her that at last she had a chance to escape.

Her first concern was to find a knife and cut her legs free. Billy Boy's Bowie knife was still in his belt. She wriggled over to him and removed it gingerly. She need not have worried, for his heavy breathing indicated the depth of his unconsciousness.

Very carefully she sawed at the rawhide until it snapped. She stood up and walked to the door. There was plenty of daylight left, if she could get astride one of the horses, she could surely put enough distance between her and these disabled men to be safe.

'Hold it!'

With a start she turned to find Levine half

sitting up, resting on one elbow, pointing his Colt at her.

'Now you wouldn't be thinkin' of going anywhere, would you, ma'am?' he said through bruised and swollen lips. 'Not when there's two guys needin' urgent treatment.'

With an effort Levine struggled to his feet. He indicated a leather bucket in the corner. 'Throw that knife down and let you and I go outside and git some water from the trough,' he said.

Under his watchful eye, Beth used the contents of the first bucket to revive Billy Boy by dousing it into his face. He groaned as he came to.

After that, it took another bucketful to clean him up. After which she made him as comfortable as she was able and stood up.

'I see you're a real genuine frontier woman, Mrs Anderson,' Levine said with undisguised admiration when she had finished cleaning his own face up and she had strapped his ribs with strips of blanket.

'I raised two brothers when Ma and Pa died,' she told him. 'I was a nurse in the war. I've seen more than just a few cuts and bruises in my time.'

Levine looked across at Billy Boy. 'Don't reckon he's gonna be any trouble to you,' he said. He folded his arms across his chest and winced. 'Any more than I will fer that matter. Even so, I gotta be sure you won't do anything foolish like trying to run away.'

'Is it true you've shot my brother?' she asked as he roped her feet and ankles together.

'You're a frontier woman, you know how it is,' Levine replied with a shrug.

* * *

Levine stirred as the first rays of sunshine slanted over the rise behind the shack. He yawned and stretched before throwing off his blanket. He experimented gingerly with the idea of getting to his feet, stifling an oath as he did so.

Beth watched him wearily from her corner. She felt unkempt and dirty after another sleepless night in the barn. Everything seemed so unreal, it seemed like a nightmare that was going on for ever.

Levine limped across to her and cut her hands loose. 'Get some hot food and coffee for us,' he grunted.

He left her feet loosely tied, compelling her to crawl on her hands and knees to do his bidding. She fed the dying embers of yesterday's fire with a few twigs and set about the task of frying bacon and boiling water for coffee.

Hearing a noise behind, she glanced over her shoulder to see Levine trying to rouse Billy Boy. He eventually succeeded.

'Bring him some coffee,' Levine ordered Beth.

As she edged across to him with a mug of the scalding liquid she noted with a nurse's professional glance the disfigurement last night's fight had wreaked on Billy Boy's face. His right eye was the colour of flowering sage, the left completely closed. Blood encrusted one enormous gash above his eye and another high on one cheek-bone. His broken nose was flattened to a smudge against his face.

'I've seen worse,' Levine remarked. He watched

as Beth eased the liquid between Billy Boy's swollen lips.

Billy Boy coughed and then took a long swig before he opened his one swollen, weeping eye.

'Why, you ornery bastard!' he snarled.

To Beth's amazement he made an effort to rise and attack Levine but the older man pushed him back contemptuously.

'Billy Boy, you got an awful lot to learn,' he said harshly. 'Now let's stop this feudin'; I got better things to do.'

'Like what?' Billy Boy croaked.

'Like I've got a meeting with the boss today.'

Beth lay quietly, listening. Someone was behind all this, after all. Who could it be?

'You gonna get paid?' Billy Boy asked Joe.

'Could be.'

'Aw, c'mon, Joe. We're pardners, you and me.'

The older man felt his ribs and winced. 'You think I trust you after what you tried to pull yesterday? I'll tell you this. If you want your cut, Billy Boy, from now on you do exactly as I say.' He rose to his feet with difficulty. 'After I've eaten, I'm ridin' out,' he said. 'You stay here and guard the woman. By the time I get back we should know where we stand.'

Beth watched Joe as he ate with mounting apprehension. She figured she was in no danger of any further assault from either man, for both of them were in too much pain from their injuries to be interested in her. But one thing was clear, Joe Levine had no intention of honouring any arrangement he had made with Billy Boy ...

As soon as he had finished eating, Levine said,

'I'm ridin' out right now.'

From the doorway, Beth watched him as he saddled his horse, mounted with difficulty, and moved out in a slow walk.

Billy Boy was sitting up when Beth came back into the cabin. 'Don't you git any ideas that I'm not able,' he told her, with a smirk. 'I got plans fer you and me.'

Beth froze.

She watched in amazement as he threw off his blanket and rose unsteadily to his feet. He was young and he was strong, for the battering Levine had given him would have laid up many another man for days.

Beth watched uneasily as Billy Boy took a few tentative steps, testing his aches and pains.

He turned and grinned. Now that Levine had left, some of his old cockiness was returning. 'I bin doin' a little figuring. I reckon Joe is planning on double-crossin' this boss of his. Well, how's about I join in the fun?'

Beth shook her head in disbelief. Billy Boy must be a fool if he thought he could double-cross a pet rabbit, but she kept the opinion to herself.

Billy Boy fastened on his gun belt, removed his Colts from their holsters and checked the loads. 'When Joe gets back, he's gonna get the surprise of his life,' he said. 'He may be good with his fists, but let's see how he is when these do the real talkin'.'

He cut Beth loose, hauled her to her feet and led her outside. The remaining horse was grazing quietly in the lush grass beside the overflow from the trough.

Billy Boy walked over to the animal and opened the saddle-bag. He returned with a scrap of paper and a stub of pencil. His brow furrowed as he struggled to write. Suddenly he lost patience, 'I cain't get the hang of this writing business,' he said. He gave Beth the paper and pencil. 'I figure you'll write a better letter than me.'

Beth waited, pencil poised.

'What do you want me to put?'

Billy Boy's face turned bright red. 'Aw hell. Just tell Joe we've gone someplace else. Say you don't come back until he comes up with ten grand,' he said.

'But ...'

'Jest do it!'

Beth rested the paper on the saddle which Billy Boy had already flung over the horse's back. She licked the pencil point and forcing her hand to keep steady, she wrote:

Billy Boy has taken me to a new location. He wants $10,000 before he will release me.

'Hey, you writin' a book or somethin?' Billy Boy snatched the paper off Beth and scowled at her flowing handwriting. 'You read it back, word fer word. And make sure you point at each one,' he demanded.

She did as he asked.

'Now get up behind me,' he said, when she had finished, 'unless you wanna walk.'

'Where are we goin'?' she asked nervously. 'Why is it necessary to leave here? Levine will only follow us ...'

'It ain't no concern of yours,' Billy Boy replied.

As soon as she had mounted behind him, he

gouged his spurs into the flank of the horse and urged it forward into the forest.

ELEVEN

A cock crowed and Brad woke to the smell of frying bacon. When he emerged dressed from behind the makeshift screen, he blinked. Miss Rossiter was formally attired in her neat grey dress, her hair was taken up and her spectacles were hanging on a silver chain round her neck.

'You're just in time, Mr Rip van Winkle,' she chided him. 'I thought I was gonna have to leave before you were awake.'

She doled out two eggs and several rashers of bacon on to a wooden platter and laid it down in front of him. 'I guess I'll have to leave you anyway?' She glanced at the timepiece on the wall. 'I'm late; would you feed the chickens fer me?'

Brad nodded. 'You reckonin' on ridin' into town alone?'

Miss Rossiter shrugged. 'I should be safe enough – it's broad daylight. Besides, we can't risk being seen together by Kroll or his cronies.'

Brad nodded.

'What you gonna do today?'

'Some more sleuthin', I guess.'

'Close ain't ya?' She sighed. 'I guess I don't blame you. The way things are I guess you don't know who to trust.'

Brad stopped eating. 'You've bin a great help, Miss Rossiter, but one thing still puzzles me. You ain't never mentioned Janelle Hawk.'

It was a stab in the dark, but it worked.

Miss Rossiter's face turned pale. 'What's she got to do with it?'

'Let me put it this way. Supposin' Janelle Hawk puts up the money, in exchange for an interest in the Double Circle. Now I reckon she's sweet on Kroll. Suppose he plans on marrying her? That way he gets the ransom money and keeps it in the family, so to speak. Where does that leave Tom Anderson?'

Miss Rossiter put the coffee pot down with a bang. Her self-assurance, once the focus of Brad's undisguised admiration, crumbled. She sat down heavily in the nearest chair and burst into tears.

Brad went over to her. 'I have to look at every angle,' he said gently. 'I guess it cain't be helped if I'm to get at the truth.'

Miss Rossiter took a neat embroidered handkerchief from the inside of her puffed sleeve and wiped her eyes. With an effort, she took command of herself.

Suddenly she faced Brad, her eyes blazing with anger. 'You knew about me and Frikki all the time, didn't you?'

'I didn't,' Brad said. 'I just figured it, that's all. So where does that leave you, Elaine?'

'You reckon I might be fittin' up Frikki because I'm jealous of his walkin' out with Janelle Hawk?'

Brad hooked both his thumbs in his vest and leaned back. 'I gotta be certain,' he said.

Vacation at San Pedro

Miss Rossiter stood up and pulled on her gloves. 'Well, figure this. I've told you I'm good friends with Beth. Check that out with anyone you like. Now it's true I'm sore over Frikki takin' up with that Hawk woman, but the plain fact is he's never made me any promises and I guess I'm too long in the tooth now to bother about it.'

She fixed Brad with a cool stare. 'You want it straight? The only guy I've ever taken a shine for is Art Crellin. I been waitin' fer years fer him to pop the question. But I reckon he's too old and set in his ways now. Frikki seduced me. Don't look so shocked, that's the right word. I guess I gave in because I needed the job. But once Frikki Kroll gets a grip on someone, he never lets go. Now, Ranger Saunders, balance the books on the evidence I've given you, and remember when you do, that Beth Anderson is the best friend I've ever had.' She turned and walked to the door. 'Now I gotta get goin' or I'll be truly late.'

Brad followed her. Outside, a horse stood stamping and snorting in the traces of a buggy.

'Miss Rossiter, I'm grateful for your hospitality. I'm real sorry for upsetting you,' he said as he helped her inside.

She took the reins and smiled at him. 'I guess you needn't be. Look, if you make up your mind in my favour, don't forget that Frikki is on the loose after lunch, will you? If you stick around the office, you can pick him up as he leaves.'

Brad nodded.

'And don't forget to feed the chickens!' she shouted back over her shoulder as she shook the reins and the buggy leapt forward.

* * *

Breakfast at the Double Circle was a sombre affair. Janelle sipped her coffee and, from the length of the massive dining-table, watched as her brother picked disconsolately at a plate of steak and eggs.

'You gotta eat somethin', Tom, you must keep your strength up,' she said softly as Tom pushed the plate away.

She paused while a coloured servant stepped forward to remove their plates. Then she said, 'I think it's time we did something. We need to ride into town and fix things with Frikki.'

'Frikki! You're always talkin' about Frikki!' Tom flared. 'As if he can wave some magic wand and bring Beth back. Oh, Janelle, I'm sorry …'

Janelle moved over to him as he put his head in his hands and his shoulders heaved with emotion. With an effort, Tom brought himself under control. 'Janelle, I've watched your relationship with Frikki growing this last few weeks …'

'I know,' Janelle replied, a dreamy look in her eyes. 'Comin' out west was the best move I've made since Wilbur died. I feel like I've come alive now I've met with Frikki.'

She stood up and walked over to the window. One of the hands rode past and lifted his hat when he saw she was watching him.

She turned back to her brother. 'I like it here in Texas. There's so much space to live in. The men show you more respect than they do back in New York.'

Tom looked at her. 'You really have taken a shine to Frikki, haven't you?' he said.

She nodded. 'Sure I have. But let's not talk anymore about me now – we gotta get Beth back, Tom, no matter what it costs.'

When he had finished feeding the chickens, Brad led his mount out of the barn, saddled up and rode out. The Double Circle ranch lay some ten miles to the north with San Pedro in between, so he judged it would be appropriate to follow Miss Rossiter along the trail to the bridge and ride on through the town.

As he rode the trail to the bridge, he instinctively kept an eye on the sign left by the passage of the buggy. But as he arrived at the bridge he drew rein.

Something was wrong!

The sign was no longer there.

His suspicions aroused, he retraced the last twenty yards, studying every inch of the way until he spotted the sign he'd missed. When he found it, he didn't like what he saw.

He scratched his head. His first priority was to locate the buggy. Where the hell had it got to? It couldn't have vanished into thin air.

Suddenly his stomach gave a lurch.

He walked to the edge of the bridge and looked down at the water foaming fifty feet below.

His worst fears were realized.

The buggy lay on its side close beside the wooden trestles, water trickling gently round it. Unless someone knew what they were looking for, it could have lain there undiscovered for weeks.

Brad glanced behind him. The bridge was built without handrails, just wide enough to permit the passage of a wagon. A careless driver who mishandled his team could easily fall over the edge. But Miss Rossiter drove her buggy this way every day of the week: she must know the trail between her cabin and San Pedro like the back of her hand.

Tense and edgy, he dismounted and, mindful of his shoulder, he climbed carefully down the slope into the creek. Standing on a rock, he cast about him. The impact had smashed the buggy to pieces. The horse lay dead in the traces, partially concealed by the wreckage.

It was a few moments before he discovered Elaine Rossiter's body. She must have been thrown clear, for she was lying several yards away, partially covered by one of the buggy's wheels. For a brief moment he thought he detected a movement, but his sudden surge of hope was short-lived.

He knew the bitter truth long before he reached the body floating gently in the shallows among the rocks.

Elaine Rossiter was dead!

Brad took a deep breath and looked away for a moment, trying to control his distress. He had seen many corpses in his time but, as long as he breathed he would never be able to come to terms with the violent death of a woman.

Closer examination revealed nothing other than the injuries caused by the fall.

Brad frowned. Was it an accident? The horse may have spooked, tipping the buggy and its occupant into the creek.

It took him several minutes of careful manoeuvring before he could release the body from the wreckage. Ignoring the pain from his shoulder, Brad picked up Elaine Rossiter's body in both arms and made his way as carefully as he could up to the trail. Once back there he took another careful look but could find no sign of any injuries other than those attributable to a heavy fall.

Puzzled, he stood back, scanning the ground thoughtfully, working outwards. After a few seconds he gave a grunt of satisfaction. Fresh hoof marks showed a rider had been waiting here recently; a pile of fresh droppings showed where his horse had been standing.

Suddenly he bethought him of his vague suspicions of the night before. He found the knoll again and scrambled up to the top. Careful scrutiny in the vicinity revealed signs of the recent passage of a man on foot and then a horse and rider.

So he had been right last night, after all!

Cursing his folly in allowing Miss Rossiter to travel alone that morning, he returned to the bridge.

Once there, he stood back and pondered. What evidence had he to prove that she had met with someone who intended to harm her?

One thing was certain – someone knew she had met with him the previous evening!

But if the observer had returned and had forced her buggy off the bridge, why wasn't there any sign of a struggle? In the short time he had known Miss Rossiter he had come to realize that she was a very fit woman; there was no way she would submit meekly to any attacker.

He shook his head in bewilderment. This was one for the County Coroner.

With reverent care, he placed the body across the waiting horse, mounted up himself, and set off at a slow walk into town.

When he arrived, he took care to avoid Commercial Street, choosing his moment circumspectly to enter by a side alley so as to avoid attracting attention. An awed youth told him where Hank Furman kept his funeral parlour.

The elderly mortician looked up in surprise when Brad entered his funeral parlour. 'Mornin', what can I do for you?' he asked with that doleful politeness that went hand-in-hand with his trade.

'Cain't think what this town's comin' to,' he muttered with a shake of his head when Brad explained the reason for his call.

'I want the County Coroner in on this one,' Brad told him.

'That's Doc Grierson,' came the reply.

'Get on to him,' Brad rapped. 'Tell him I'd appreciate a report on the cause of death by midday.'

'Sure thing,' Hank Furman replied.

'Hank, I gotta feelin' there's more to come,' Brad warned him. 'Meantime I'd be obliged if you'll keep your mouth shut on this one fer the time bein'.'

Relieved of his sad chore, Brad rode out on to Commercial Street. As he passed Kroll's office, he looked neither right nor left, his face set hard. From what Miss Rossiter had told him, there was no doubt in his mind now that Kroll was the man behind all this. It was difficult to resist the temptation to stop by and blow him apart. But his only witness was dead and what good would it do when he still had no idea of Beth's whereabouts?

An hour later, he rode through the gates of the Double Circle Ranch.

Art Crellin spotted his arrival and appeared from the bunkhouse to greet him.

'Howdy, how's things?' the big man asked hopefully.

Brad shook his head. Mindful of what Elaine Rossiter had told him of Crellin's interest in her, he preferred to keep the news of her death to himself for the moment: he dare not risk Crellin taking the law into his own hands, there was too much at stake.

'Looks like the General's gonna have to sell out if you don't come up with somethin' pretty soon,' Crellin said as he fell in beside Brad.

Brad stopped and eyed him balefully. 'You reckon I ain't gonna find my sister?' he growled.

Crellin turned pale under his tan. 'No offence intended, but time is runnin' out.'

The children waylaid Brad as soon as he crossed the threshold.

'You found our ma yet?' George piped plaintively.

'Of course he hasn't, bonehead,' Hannah said scornfully.

'How do you know?' George demanded.

"Cos he ain't brought her with him, has he?'

'I want my ma back.'

Brad's heart turned over to see the boy's distress. It brought back bitter memories of the day brother Clem had found his father's body out on the range, scalped and with an arrow through his back. When Clem had ridden in with his father's mutilated body he had been physically sick.

'Shush there, my baby.' A coloured servant rushed forward to console the little boy.

'I ain't a-weepin',' George said manfully. 'Pa says weepin' is women's work.'

'That you Brad?' Tom's voice called from the open door to his study. He limped forward, resting on his stick. 'Any news?'

When Brad shook his head, his face turned grim. 'Take the children away,' he snapped at the servant. 'I got things to discuss with my brother-in-law.'

'Can I be in on this?'

Brad turned to see Janelle Hawk approaching them. She seemed an oasis of calm in this troubled household.

'Sure. Best we talk in my study,' Tom said.

Once the three of them were inside, Tom closed the door and turned to Brad. 'Well?'

Brad felt Janelle Hawk's eyes settle on him. This was no time for parading his suspicions, he decided. 'Have to be honest, Tom,' he said. 'This one's tough.'

'No progress?'

Brad shook his head.

Tom opened a box of cigars and passed one to Brad. The latter struck a lucifer and lit the cigarette Janelle had produced from a silver-chased box. As he did so, their eyes met but the deep, dark pools that were Janelle's told him nothing. If she was playing some deep game with Kroll, she showed no sign of it. But then, Brad had to admit, dealing with beautiful conniving women wasn't exactly his specialty.

The flame flickered just long enough to light the

men's cigars.

Tom waited until his cigar was drawing evenly, then he said: 'I think I'm gonna have to take up Janelle's offer to buy into the Double Circle, Brad.'

'You know I'm only too pleased to help, Tom,' she said.

'You've made that quite clear,' Tom replied. 'And I gotta say how grateful I am.'

'When do you propose to fix the deal?' Brad asked.

'We discussed it this morning at breakfast,' Janelle said. 'Look, Tom, I'll level with you, I've already wired my bank in New York to authorize the sale of sufficient securities to guarantee the shipment of the money from Austin.'

'You've done what?' Tom exclaimed.

'It will arrive by train at four o'clock tomorrow afternoon. I've sent a message to Frikki to that effect asking for a meeting with him. We'll sign the legal documents, collect the money, and pay off Beth's ransom.'

Tom bit his lip.

Brad rose. 'That gives me twenty-four hours to find Beth. I'd best get movin',' he said grimly.

'Good luck, Ranger Saunders.' Janelle Hawk smiled as she spoke.

Tom limped after Brad to the door. When they were alone, he clamped his hand on Brad's arm. 'I only wish I could ride with you,' he said harshly. 'Whatever happens, I want Beth back. Money isn't important now. I don't care if it costs me every cent I own.'

Brad left the Double Circle in a thoughtful mood. A noose was being slowly drawn round Tom

Anderson's ownership of the Double Circle, he was convinced of that.

He rode back into town just after midday and called in on Doc Grierson.

'Hank told me you were suspicious about the cause of Elaine Rossiter's death,' the doctor said. His eyes gleamed with professional interest. 'I reckon I got somethin' for you. Come through and have a look.'

Brad followed him through to a room at the back of the house. Once inside, Doc Grierson closed the door and walked over to the bench where the body lay under a sheet.

Using a pair of forceps, Doc Grierson picked up a small piece of metal from a Petri dish. He held it out for Brad to inspect.

'A slug?' Brad's eyebrows raised. 'And a small one, too.'

'Right,' said Doc. 'Now take a look at this.'

Brad followed him over to the corpse. Doc Grierson whipped back the sheet and held up the head, turning it sideways so that Brad could see the area where he had shaved away the hair to expose what had once been a neat round entry hope, widened somewhat as a result of Doc Grierson's probing.

'She was shot from close range with a small calibre bullet, most probably from a vest-pocket type of pistol,' Doc Grierson said briskly as he covered the body again.

'A .28 derringer, maybe?' Brad suggested.

Doc Grierson nodded. 'Something like that. There are extensive injuries consistent with a heavy fall from a great height. But it's my opinion

Vacation at San Pedro

that Elaine Rossiter was shot first from close range before the fall. She was dead before she hit the creek.' Doc Grierson's mouth compressed to a hyphen as he showed the first crack in his professional reserve. 'Now who the hell would want to do a thing like this to Elaine?'

'You've done your bit, Doc,' Brad told him. 'Leave the rest to me.'

Doc Grierson studied Brad. 'You must be tough to be up and about. How's that shoulder feel?'

'Painful. But not as bad as the first time it happened. Now if you'll excuse me, Doc, I got this business to attend to.'

Brad rode on into town and hitched his horse outside the Golden Fleece. The barkeep served him beer without remark, for trade was brisk.

Brad toyed with the idea of asking more questions, but rejected it. He found him a seat by the window where he could keep his eyes on Kroll's office. Never in his life had he felt so frustrated. He had downed one beer and was half-way through the second when the door opened and Kroll appeared to meet with an old-timer limping along, leading a big bay from the direction of the livery stables.

Brad left his drink and made his way outside, just in time to see Kroll cantering along the street.

Following his man was the least of his problems. Clearly Kroll was a city man, obviously unconcerned that someone should be taking an interest in his movements. What concerned him more was the man Kroll was meeting with.

The trail led out of town and through thick forest. Brad continued to ride as perceptively as an Indian, always keeping his man in view, yet never allowing himself to be seen.

About two miles out of town, a rider suddenly emerged from the trees and confronted Kroll. As he craned his neck to see, Brad exhaled a sigh of satisfaction. Elaine Rossiter had not let him down ...

TWELVE

From the way the approaching horse skitted and pranced, Brad sensed the oncoming rider was wary – and he was sitting the animal awkwardly, as though he was injured in some way. At fifty paces it was impossible to hear what the two men were saying, but Brad had no intention of trying to get closer. Kroll seemed cool enough, but the other man's highly-strung condition meant that the slightest dislodging of a pebble could spook him. The risk of attempting to move closer in simply wasn't worth it.

As the new arrival dismounted, Brad noted he was an older man. As the seconds passed, he became more and more certain that he was Joe Levine.

After a few minutes of animated conversation, Kroll took a stout manilla envelope from his saddle-bag and passed it to Levine. The meeting came to an abrupt end and Kroll was the first to remount his horse and retrace his way along the trail back to San Pedro.

Levine watched him until he was out of sight before he too, remounted, turned round, and rode off in the opposite direction.

Brad rose cautiously from his hiding-place and remounted his horse. At all costs, he must not let Levine out of his sight.

But this man proved to be the hardest quarry Brad had ever tracked in his life. He rode through the seemingly endless forest in such a manner that his presence was concealed beyond a distance of a few yards and Brad was forced to hang well back, trying to keep his distance, yet keep in touch without revealing his own presence.

His care and patience were rewarded for, by the time Levine reached the barn, Brad was certain the man had no idea he was being followed.

Brad reined in, dismounted and tethered his horse well out of sight. He paused to check his weapon and then he edged stealthily forward from tree to tree, until he could see the barn.

But even as he settled down to watch, he felt his guts cramp.

The barn was empty!

He did not need Levine's volley of curses to confirm it.

He watched dispassionately as Levine reappeared, holding a scrap of paper. The outlaw read it and then ripped it up, scattering the pieces on the ground, uttering another curse as he did so. Then he began to prowl around the barn, obviously casting about for sign.

Brad deduced that Levine's angry reaction stemmed from the fact that his partner must have double-crossed him. If Beth wasn't inside the barn, then the other man must have removed her elsewhere. He smiled grimly to himself. Never yet had he seen any code of honour maintained

Vacation at San Pedro

between the vicious breed of men on whom he waged constant war.

Levine's thorough and systematic search was rewarded for in less than ten minutes the ex-convict had remounted his horse and headed out into the forest.

Brad darted out of his hiding-place to rescue the torn scraps of paper already scattering in the breeze. Piecing it together, he read the message. His spirits rose as he recognized Beth's handwriting.

He made a brief check inside the barn. The smell of rats and the swarm of flies buzzing round a small pile of trash was sufficient proof of recent occupation.

But now the most difficult part so far began. The tracker still had to be tracked. Two things were going for Brad. One was that Levine was so absorbed in his task that he had no thought now for being followed himself; the other was that there was no need for him to hang in too close for the trail left by Beth's captor couldn't have been clearer if it had been blazed through the forest with an axe.

After a few minutes, Brad paused to inspect a torn fragment of cloth hanging from a twig. It could only be from Beth's dress. He felt another surge of optimism. Apart from the note, this was the only hard evidence he had that Beth had passed this way.

His hand moved to his weapon. All his instincts told him to overtake the man ahead, kill him and take over this ludicrously simple piece of tracking. The only thing that stopped him was the thought that Beth might not be far away and the sound of a gunshot would warn her captor.

Brad forced himself to relax. Sooner or later, the outlaw ahead must meet up with his sidekick. Then, *then* he knew he must use all the advantage surprise could give him to overcome the two men and recover Beth. And if that meant that both of them had to die then, in McNelly's own ruthless words, 'So be it'.

After several miles of rough riding through the forest, Beth's dress was tattered and torn beyond recognition. The sun was past its height when they emerged out of the trees into the hilly, broken country which led down to the river.

They rode on for another two hours until Billy Boy came to a halt beside the base of a rock-strewn hill.

Beth watched as he dismounted. A more desolate place she could not imagine. Just what was this crazy boy trying to achieve?

'I guess this here'll do,' Billy Boy said, squinting at the sun.

'What in the world are you thinkin' of?' Beth whispered through cracked and swollen lips. 'We've left a trail behind us wider than the Chisholm.'

Billy Boy uttered his unnaturally high-pitched laugh. 'You're gonna find out soon,' he said as he unhooked his canteen and took a swig of water. Then he poured some into his hat and offered it to his horse. When he finished he put the canteen away without offering any to Beth. She closed her eyes in desperation, her lips moving in a silent

Vacation at San Pedro

prayer for help.

Billy Boy removed the rope that secured her to the horse and led her into the rocks. He found a spot in a cleft and pushed her roughly to the ground and bound her legs.

'You stay here, outa sight,' he said. 'And jest to be sure you don't squawk I'll stop yore mouth.'

With that he removed his sweat-stained bandanna and gagged her with it. When he had finished, he stood back to survey his handiwork.

'Hell, look at yuh. Who in the world would think you was worth a fortune?' he sneered.

He went over to the horse, removed his Winchester and checked the loads. He cocked one eye on the sun. 'Well, now I guess I'll get me some practice in ransomin',' he said with a grin.

He had left Beth lying face down. With an effort she managed to roll over on to her side so that she could see her captor climbing one of the rocks that overlooked the way they had come. In a haze of weakness and pain, it suddenly came over Beth as to what Billy Boy was about.

He wanted Levine to find him!

Billy Boy must think he had the situation within his control and was on ground of his own choosing. His plan was as transparent as varnish, he was going to kill Levine and take any money the man might have in his possession. The youthful Billy Boy was learning fast ...

The sun was standing half-mast in the sky when Brad finally trailed Levine to the nondescript outcrop. Here, the forest had thinned dramatically and the outcrop was the only distinctive landmark in the landscape.

Levine too seemed to think their journey was at an end, for he had stopped. Brad spent an uneasy few moments waiting while the man decided what to do.

Brad's patience finally gave out. It was time to take control of events now, rather than submit to them. Keeping the outcrop in sight, Brad eased away to circle right of Levine, hoping to get a clear view of what was about to happen.

When it came, the blast of a rifle shot made him rein in his mount. He jumped down and cast about until he found some dead ground where he could tether the animal safely out of sight. That done, he dived forward on to his belly and crawled forward until he could see what was happening.

'That's far enough!'

The shout came from the rocks.

After a few seconds, another shot rang out and Levine hastily whirled round his horse through a hundred and eighty degrees back into cover.

After a few moments, Levine waved his bandanna. 'You an' me need to talk, Billy Boy!'

When there was no reply, Levine shouted, 'I know you're peeved 'bout yesterday, but get a grip on yourself, there's things we gotta get straight.'

'I know that,' Billy Boy shouted. 'That's why I brought the woman out here with me. This way *you* gotta listen.'

While the two men were thus engaged, Brad used the opportunity to crawl closer and closer.

'I woulda listened anyway,' Levine shouted. 'There was no need fer this wild goose chase.'

'Oh yeah? I guess we'll see about that,' Billy Boy

Vacation at San Pedro

replied.

Brad emerged at the base of the outcrop on the opposite side to where the two men were haggling.

'Look, Billy Boy, I've got five grand in my saddle-bags. Turns out I didn't kill the ranger after all. We've gotta move fast or it's no dice.'

With the greatest of care, Brad manoeuvred his way round until Billy Boy came into sight. The young outlaw had his back to Brad. Negotiations were coming to an end for he stood up as though to meet Levine.

'Come on, Billy Boy. One thing you gotta learn is patience. If you'd just done five years like I have, you'd know what I mean. You an' me can take all the money iffen we play our cards right.'

At that moment Brad saw Beth lying bound and gagged in a hollow basin of rocks. He restrained the urge to rush to her aid, for the meeting between the two men on the rim of rock had to be his prime concern. He moved stealthily from rock to rock until he had a clear view of Levine's approach.

'I guessed you'd see it my way,' Levine said as he drew closer.

From his hiding-place in the rocks, Brad saw Billy Boy standing, legs astride, holding his rifle at high port, awaiting Levine's approach.

Twenty yards away, Levine stopped to catch his breath. 'That was some fight we had, Billy Boy,' he grinned. 'But now we're pardners I guess. That's what you always wanted, wasn't it?'

Levine scrambled upwards again, narrowing the distance between himself and Billy Boy to twenty yards. 'Shore could do with some chuck and a rest,' he said.

'That's far enough!' Billy Boy pointed his Winchester at Levine.

Levine grinned. 'Aw c'mon Billy Boy, I'm gettin' too old fer these kinda games.'

'This ain't no game, Joe.' Billy Boy's high-pitched laugh echoed off the rocks. 'I got you chasin' me, and now I aim to finish yuh.'

Levine's face turned red with anger. 'Billy Boy, what's eatin' yuh? Like I said, we'll split fifty-fifty. You cain't do nuthin' without me.'

'Jest try me! Why should I split with you when I kin go fer the jackpot?'

Levine laughed harshly. 'That's crazy talk! Look, I've levelled with ya. That ranger ain't dead. He's on the prod and gettin' closer by the minute. All we gotta do is hold the woman until this time tomorrow. Then we take all the money and run.'

'No way!'

'C'mon, Billy Boy. I'm callin' the shots an' I'm tellin' yuh, don't try to be clever.'

'While I've got the woman, I'm callin' the shots,' Billy Boy said stubbornly. He raised the rifle. 'I reckon I cin take what you're gonna get and up the stakes.'

'How can yuh? You don't even know who you're dealin' with. And if that ranger gits any closer, yore dead.'

'You've gone yella, Joe. That ranger don't scare me none. Why, I can call him out any day.'

'Don't be a fool, Billy Boy. Killin' a drunken cowpoke in Austin don't make you a gunfighter.'

Billy Boy threw the rifle aside and widened his stance. His hands hovered like hawk's claws over the butts of his Colts. 'You reckon?' he said. His voice rose to a higher pitch. 'So make yore play, smartass and be my second notch.'

If Levine felt fear, he showed no sign of it. He took a step forward. He jerked his thumb over his shoulder. 'Like I said, I got money in my saddle-bag back there. Half is yours. Now quit actin' loco. For Gawd's sake let's get together, grab the money an' get out of Pegg County.'

'Draw, damn you, draw!'

At this moment, Brad stepped out of his hiding-place and drew his Colt. 'Hold it!' he said.

Levine and Billy Boy half-turned. When they saw Brad their mouths sagged open in disbelief.

'Gawd Almighty, the ranger!' Levine exclaimed.

Brad saw Billy Boy's eyes narrow. This crazy kid was going to make his play, even though he had the drop on him.

As Billy Boy's hands forked for his weapons, Brad took no chances. With all the advantage of an already drawn weapon, Brad was able to fire a disabling shot. The bullet from his Colt slammed into Billy Boy's left forearm, forcing him to drop one of his weapons with a clatter onto the rocks.

'You lousy sonofabitch!' Billy Boy howled in agony as a jet of blood spurted from the flesh wound in his left forearm.

He raised his other weapon, but Brad stepped forward and in a single rapid movement, smashed his right arm down with the barrel of his Colt, knocking the weapon down.

'Lesson number one,' Brad said. 'Never draw when a guy has the drop on you.'

Levine backed off, hands held high.

'Down here.' Brad indicated the spot where Beth lay trussed as he spoke. When Billy Boy hesitated Brad put his foot into the small of his back and gave him a shove that sent him sprawling headlong among the jagged rocks.

'I said move!' he snarled.

The two men scrambled down to where Beth lay.

'Rope this halfwit up,' Brad ordered Levine.

'He's bleedin' like a stuck pig,' Levine complained.

'Then tie a knot round his arm,' Brad said. 'That'll keep him alive for now.'

When Levine had finished Brad stepped forward and in one swift movement clubbed him with the Colt, dropping him like a sack of potatoes on to the ground in front of Billy Boy. That gave Brad ample time to secure his second prisoner.

Only then did he feel confident enough to release Beth.

He took out his Bowie and released the gag. Her lips were dry and cracked and her tongue swollen for lack of water so that she couldn't speak straight away.

'Beth,' he whispered hoarsely. 'What the hell did they do to ya?'

A great rage tore through Brad. Without waiting for an answer, he straightened up, drew his Colt and walked over to where his two prisoners lay.

'No, Brad!'

Even though Beth's voice was only a croak it still carried the old force of authority he remembered from his youth.

Vacation at San Pedro

Slowly he holstered the weapon and returned to the task of unfastening the bonds that dug so cruelly into his sister's wrists and ankles.

When she was free he embraced her, trying hard to check the emotion that welled up inside him.

'Why Brad, that ain't a little bitty tear in your eye, is it?' she whispered as she massaged her stiff limbs.

He turned away to compose himself before he gave her another squeeze. That was Beth, always self-possessed. He brought her water.

'That crack-brained kid might have figured he could, but we can't stay here the night,' he said. 'There ain't nuthin' fer the horses. Iffen you can ride there's time to get back to that old barn before sundown. Then tomorrow first light we'll get you back home. You reckon you can ride?'

'I just bin to hell an' back. Sure, I cin ride,' Beth assured him.

Brad sighed with relief. Leaving his sister to recover in her own time, he set out to collect his own horse and Levine's. He recovered the envelope which Kroll had given Levine. Inspection revealed it contained a thousand dollars in high demonination greenbacks and not the five thousand Levine had told Billy Boy.

When he returned, he forced his prisoners to mount two to a horse, roping their legs together under the animal's belly. He gave the other horse to Beth, helped her into the saddle and mounted his own.

'Brad, who is behind all this?' Beth asked when they were moving.

'Kroll,' he replied.

Beth bit her lip. 'Well, of all the double-crossin' sidewinders! Just wait while I get my hands on him,' she said venomously.

'Don't *soil* your hands,' Brad said. 'Leave him to me.'

They made the journey in silence back to the barn. It was gathering dusk when they arrived. Brad made Beth as comfortable as he could before he gave his prisoners some water.

'I'm delivering you to the San Pedro jail tomorrow,' he told the pair of them. 'It shoulda been the morticians. You got my sister to thank fer that.'

As dawn broke, Brad had his prisoners back in the saddle.

He took Beth to one side. 'We're ridin' back via the Double Circle. With any luck we might get there before Tom has gone into San Pedro with Janelle.'

'Why should he do that?' Beth enquired.

'The money to ransom you is arrivin' on the afternoon train from Austin. Janelle's made that possible.'

Beth nodded. 'That's real good of her,' she said. 'I appreciate that.'

Brad was about to voice his misgivings, but he thought the better of it.

Beth was drooping in the saddle by the time they reached the Double Circle. Crellin's whoop of delight brought the cowhands erupting from the bunkhouse to greet them.

'OK, fellas, quit the celebratin', there's work to do,' Brad said curtly as he dismounted. The men

Vacation at San Pedro

fell into a respectful silence as he spoke. 'I take it General Anderson has already left for San Pedro?' he asked Crellin.

The big foreman nodded. 'Sure. He took Mrs Hawk with him.'

Brad remounted. 'Take Mrs Anderson inside and get the servants to make her comfortable. After that bring these prisoners into town and lock them in the jail.'

'It'll be a pleasure,' Crellin said. He waited while Beth had left them. Then he took a closer look at Levine and said, 'Say ain't he the gambler that did for Pete after that poker game?'

When Brad nodded, Crellin said, 'Say, how about these guys meet with an accident on the way into town? Somethin' like they tried to escape and we shot them?' he said with a wink.

There was a murmur of approval from the assembled men. 'Shootin's too easy,' one of them said. 'I reckon stringin' up is all them bastards is fit fer.'

Brad held up his hand for silence. 'My job is upholdin' the law. These men are my prisoners and I'm entrustin' you with the task of bringin' 'em in. I'm gonna ride ahead into San Pedro as fast as I can – the future of the Double Circle is at stake. Need I say more?'

Crellin hesitated. 'You're the boss,' he said.

Without another word, Brad kick-started his horse into a headlong dash along the trail into town.

THIRTEEN

Brad tore along Commercial Street and did a running dismount outside Kroll's office. He tossed a coin at a young lad lounging on the boardwalk. 'Take care of my hoss,' he snapped as he strode towards the door of the building without waiting for a reply.

He took the stairs to Miss Rossiter's office two at a time and thrust open the door. He paused, listening intently. The murmur of voices from the room within told him the meeting was in progress. He walked straight across to the door and entered without knocking.

Tom Anderson was leaning over Kroll's desk, pen in hand. Janelle was standing beside him. Kroll was sitting behind his desk watching them.

'Tom, don't you sign anything!' Brad rapped.

His brother-in-law eased back from the desk, the ink wet on his pen. His face turned grim. 'Why, Brad, what are you thinking of, burstin' in here this way?' he said.

'I'm stoppin' you from signin' away the Double Circle,' Brad replied.

Kroll stared at Brad, his face a mask of arrogance. 'This is preposterous, Ranger Saunders! Mr Anderson is taking the necessary steps to ransom his wife. The money is arriving this afternoon. Mr Anderson is signing now in order to expedite matters. I must warn you that any delay could have the most serious repercussions.'

'Fine words, Mr Lawyer Man,' Brad said. 'The only person who is facin' repercussions is *you*.'

Tom frowned. 'I can only hope you can justify this intrusion, Brad,' he said. He took out his watch and consulted it. 'Time is runnin' out. The exchange for Beth is due at six. Once we've finished here, we're going to the station to pick up the money.'

'I got Beth back this afternoon. She's safe at the ranch.'

'Wha ... at?'

Tom and Janelle stared at Brad as though he were a mighty conjuror. The only person who remained completely unmoved was Kroll.

'I found her in some very bad company,' Brad continued. His eyes locked on to Kroll as he spoke. 'Known to you, I believe. A guy named Joe Levine and his sidekick, Billy Boy Morgan.'

'Joe Levine!' Tom found his voice at last. He banged his fist on the desk. 'Of course! His five years is up.'

Janelle took a step forward to confront Brad. 'Who is this man, Levine?' she demanded. 'And what did you mean when you said Mr Kroll knew him?'

'Let me explain, Janelle,' Kroll intervened smoothly before Brad could reply. 'Five years ago I defended this man Levine against a charge brought by Tom that he had assaulted and seriously injured one of his men. I was only doin' my job. Tom and I disagreed over this one. I lost and Levine has served his sentence.'

'And came out feeling the need for revenge,' Tom said gravely.

'Exactly. Such men deprave the west,' Kroll went on smoothly. 'They are so crude in their methods I wonder why I bother with them.'

'I couldn't agree more,' said Tom.

'Tom – you and I have always been rivals but we remain the best of friends.' Kroll leaned back and spread his arms wide. 'Why, see now, look how I've been doin' my best to help.'

Tom shook hands with Brad. 'I guess I just can't thank you enough for gettin' Beth back for me.' He turned back to Kroll. 'Look, I'm sorry the deal's gotta be off, Frikki, I have to get back to Beth ...'

Kroll held up his hands in an understanding gesture. 'Sure, sure, Tom. I'm just so pleased everything's turned out right for you.'

'Hold it, Tom,' Brad snapped. 'Sure, Levine had a motive – but Kroll was his motivator.'

As Kroll leaned forward, Brad saw the knuckles of both hands were white as he rested his chin on the bridge he made with both hands. 'Now just what do you mean by that, Ranger Saunders?' he said quietly.

Tom's smiling face became serious. 'This is a serious accusation, Brad. What evidence do you have to support it?'

'OK, let's make a start by asking Mr Kroll what's happened to Elaine Rossiter,' Brad said.

'My clerk?' Kroll spread his hands wide. 'Why, I guess she hasn't turned in these last two days.

Maybe she's sick. Never known it before, I must say.'

'Never missed work before and you didn't think fit to enquire? I wonder why?'

'Ranger Saunders, I am not here to be lectured by you ...'

'I found her body yesterday morning lying at the foot of the bridge over Alexander's Creek,' Brad went on smoothly.

'You – you mean Elaine's dead?' Tom gasped.

Brad nodded. 'Doc Grierson did an autopsy and signed the death certificate.'

Kroll sat back, his face impassive. 'It must have been an accident,' he said flatly.

'It was no accident. She was shot in the back of the head from close range before she was dumped with the hoss and buggy into the creek.'

Janelle covered her face with her hands. 'How awful!' she exclaimed.

'And is this connected in some way with Beth's abduction?' Tom asked Brad.

'Sure,' Brad replied. Never taking his eyes off Kroll he continued, 'Yesterday, after your meeting here, Miss Rossiter sent me a note requesting to see me ...'

'There isn't a grain of truth in this,' Kroll cut in. 'If Miss Rossiter sent you a note it would be because she ...' he coughed embarrassedly. 'Well, I guess it's because she was that type of woman.'

Brad restrained the urge to ball his fist and smash it into Kroll's face. But he kept his temper. If he lost his temper now Kroll would win in the eyes of Tom and Janelle. Somehow, someway, he was determined to break this man down.

'Someone trailed us out to the meeting place,' Brad went on.

Kroll stifled a yawn. 'Ranger Saunders, there is no need for you to fill in the details of this sordid business.'

Brad went on doggedly, 'When we met, she informed me of your meeting with the sheriff and Levine. She had figured you were involved in Beth's abduction and informed me that you were to have a secret meeting with Joe Levine yesterday afternoon.'

'Now wait a minute, that can't be right,' Tom Anderson stepped forward.

'Will you let me finish?' Brad snapped. 'First, Kroll knew she had contacted me. He would have liked to bushwhack the pair of us at the bridge but I reckon he didn't have the know-how or the guts fer it.'

'I don't believe a word of this!' Janelle cried.

'Be careful what you say, Ranger Saunders,' Kroll said. 'So far, you haven't produced a shred of evidence to support this wild accusation.'

Brad drove on remorselessly. 'Second, I trailed you yesterday afternoon. You met with Levine.' Here, Brad produced the envelope from inside his shirt and emptied the greenbacks on to Kroll's desk. 'And gave him this money and further instructions.'

The room fell silent for a few seconds.

'I trailed Levine all the way until I found Beth holed-up with his half-witted sidekick who was tryin' some mad idea of his own.'

'This is nothing but a pack of lies!' Kroll's voice rose for the first time. 'Your word against mine!

You're a liar, Saunders!' He looked at Tom Anderson and Janelle. 'He can prove absolutely nothing against me.'

'You thought you'd get away with it if you murdered your only material witness – Elaine Rossiter,' Brad said. 'You never bargained on me catching up with Levine. One thing's certain – he won't go down without bringin' you with him ...'

Brad stopped in mid-sentence as Kroll's hand dived for his vest pocket. It was no contest. Brad's Colt appeared in his hand before Kroll had time to pull his derringer.

'Drop it,' Brad said.

As it clattered on to the desk, Brad reached forward, picked it up, broke it open and inspected it.

'This is the .28 model.' He sniffed at the barrel. 'It's bin fired recently,' he said.

Beads of sweat began to form on Kroll's forehead.

Brad looked round at his audience. 'Doc Grierson told me Miss Rossiter was shot at close range – by a small calibre slug,' he said. 'Just such a one as might have been fired by this weapon.'

'Now just a minute, Brad. Are you quite sure you have this thing right?' Tom Anderson asked.

Brad ignored him. He pocketed the weapon. 'Kroll, I'm arrestin' you on charges of abduction and murder ...'

'No!'

Brad took a pace backwards as Janelle darted forward, but before he could react, she had knocked his gun arm down.

By the time Brad recovered, Kroll had leapt

over the desk seized Janelle and, using her as a screen, backed away through the door.

Before he left the Double Circle, Art Crellin divided his hands into two groups. One half he left to guard Mrs Anderson, the other half rode alongside him into San Pedro, keeping the two sullen prisoners in their midst.

'What the hell do you want?' Sheriff Ryan barked when Crellin entered his office.

'The keys to your cells,' the ranch foreman replied. 'I got two prisoners the ranger wants lookin' after.'

Ryan grabbed a bottle and took a long pull at it. His jaw dropped as Crellin's men ushered Levine and Billy Boy into his office.

'Mrs Anderson's abductors,' Crellin said laconically. 'If I'd had my way they'd be hangin' from the nearest tree by now – and so would you.'

Levine scowled Ryan into silence as Crellin cut the outlaws loose from their bonds, unlocked the cells and pushed them unceremoniously inside. He locked up and tossed the keys on to the desk. 'Best look after those,' he said to Ryan. 'Otherwise your miserable life won't be worth livin'.'

Outside, Crellin tilted his stetson and scratched his balding head. He summoned his men about him and said, 'Listen boys, I got a little business on in town.'

'Shore is hot, Boss, cain't we have a drink to pass the time?' one guy said.

'OK,' said Crellin genially.

'You gonna see Miss Rossiter?' A tall cowboy asked, his gums showed in a horse-faced grin as he spoke.

Crellin's face turned red with embarrassment.

'Why don't you go pop the question, Art?' the tall cowboy teased.

'OK, OK,' Crellin held his hands up for silence. 'Go and have a drink, boys, but just stick together, will ya?'

'Why, Boss, will you be needin' help?' a young cowhand, scarcely sixteen, piped up.

Crellin's great boom led the ensuing shout of laughter.

He waited while the men trooped off in the direction of the Golden Fleece, straightened his bandanna and stetson, checked his reflection out in a shop window and set off across the street towards Lawyer Kroll's office.

Crellin and his men had scarcely been gone for a minute before Levine was hollering at Ryan through the bars of the cell. 'C'mon, you drunken ole bum, you let us outta here, ya hear?'

Ryan took another swig from the bottle. He was sweating profusely. Suddenly he slumped forward in his chair.

'Will ya look at the sonofabitch?' Billy Boy said incredulously. 'He's fallen asleep.'

Levine shook his head in disgust. As he did so, his eyes fell on a pail in the corner of the cell. A cursory inspection showed it to be just over half full of stale urine.

Even the coarse-minded Billy Boy wrinkled his nose in disgust as Ryan picked it up.

'I'm getting too close to a return visit to Austin Penitentiary to be partic'lar,' Levine said. 'We got us some hard talkin' to do, Billy Boy.'

He hoisted the slop pail waist high and eyed the distance between himself and the desk where Ryan lay slumped. He drew the pail back.

'Maybe this'll do fer starters ...'

The contents of the pail roused Ryan immediately.

'Now come on, you old fool, give me them keys,' Levine growled.

Ryan pawed his streaming face. 'Why should I? If the ranger finds I've let you out, there'll be hell to pay.'

'There'll be worse if you don't,' Levine said darkly. 'You think we're gonna go to jail without takin' you with us? You're in this, Ryan, right up to yore neck.'

Ryan's hand slid slowly towards the keys.

'Now that's talkin',' Billy Boy chipped in. He eyed the gun racks on the wall. 'You got plenty of hardware here. You let us go and we'll see the ranger don't live to tell any tales 'bout you, me or anyone else fer that matter. Besides which, there's a heap of money arrivin' in town soon.'

Levine clapped Billy Boy on the shoulder. 'Well, now, that's about the most sensible thing I ever heard you say.'

Crellin had scarcely made ten yards along the sidewalk when he met with his old friend Hank Furman.

'Cain't stop now, Hank,' Crellin bustled by impatiently.

But Hank held on to his arm. 'Hold it, Art, I got somethin' to tell ya.'

'OK, but make it quick,' Crellin said. He eyed Hank speculatively. 'Hell man, you look as if you've seen a ghost. I allus reckoned that too much dealin' with corpses ain't good fer a man.'

Hank drew so close that Crellin could smell the odour of death on his clothes. 'Listen, Art, the ranger brought one in early yesterday morning.'

'Yesterday mornin'? I saw him later and he said nuthin'.'

'He swore me to secrecy, but I reckon you, above all people, has gotta right to know 'bout this one.'

Crellin's deeply tanned face turned pale. 'What you sayin', Hank?' he said hoarsely. 'C'mon, man, spit it out.'

'It's Elaine Rossiter,' Hank replied. 'The ranger found her body tipped over the bridge into Alexander's Creek. Doc Grierson did an autopsy. She'd been shot in the head from behind.'

Crellin slumped back against the wall for support. All the colour drained from his face. 'I ... I don't believe it,' he said hoarsely.

Hank nodded. 'I'm sorry, Art, I truly am.'

Crellin took a deep breath, channelling his anguish into rage instead of grief. 'I saw the ranger earlier today – he never said a word 'bout it,' he muttered.

'I laid her out real nice, Art. Feel free to come and see her, any time,' Hank said.

Crellin swayed on his feet momentarily.

Hank grabbed his arm. 'Come and have a drink with me, Art. You look as though you need one.'

Crellin ignored his friend's plea.

'Sorry Hank, there's things I gotta do.' Without another word to his friend, he hitched his gunbelt and strode across the street.

Two minutes later, as he arrived outside the door of Kroll's offices, at the top of the stairs, Crellin was totally unprepared for what happened next.

The door burst open and Kroll backed through, towing Janelle Hawk.

Knocked off balance, Crellin toppled backwards downstairs. As Kroll scrambled past him, he bent down and snatched the Colt from Crellin's holster. Then he slammed the outer door behind him and pushed Janelle ahead of him out into the street.

FOURTEEN

As Kroll backed into the street, one arm locked round Janelle's waist, Levine and Billy Boy spilled out of Sheriff Ryan's office, cockahoop and armed to the teeth with Colts and Winchesters taken from Sheriff Ryan's gun racks.

When Brad arrived in the street, he found his way blocked by the two outlaws covering Kroll's withdrawal with a hail of lead.

'One move from you, Ranger, and the woman dies!' Kroll shouted, holding Crellin's Colt to her neck.

Brad dropped to the ground, rolling over and over, as Levine raised his Winchester and emptied the magazine at him.

From the corner of a stationary wagon wheel, Brad saw that Kroll was a hundred yards away by now, still holding Janelle close to him. As the townspeople rushed for cover, Levine and Billy Boy used the confusion to follow Kroll, dragging two mounts apiece they'd seized from the Double Circle horses tethered outside the Golden Fleece.

At this point, Crellin's men erupted out of the saloon and loosed a fusillade of shots down the street at the fleeing outlaws.

'Hold your fire, boys!' Brad bawled at them. 'They've got Mrs Hawk with them!'

Tom Anderson limped out on to the stoop. 'Brad, we can't let Kroll and his hoodlums get away with this,' he called out.

As the fugitives disappeared down a side alley leading off Commercial Street, Brad was aware of the ring of anxious faces gathering around him. No one spoke – it was as if they turned to him instinctively for leadership.

The street began to buzz with activity once more as the danger passed and people emerged from their hiding-places. Brad rose and walked across to Tom Anderson. He took him on one side. 'You sure you want that, Tom? Way I see it, Janelle could be in league with Kroll.'

Tom drew back. 'Why, Brad, whatever makes you think that?'

'Don't let me hear you talk that way, Brad Saunders!'

Brad whirled round to see Beth looking down at him from a majestic white stallion. Their horses panting and flecked with foam from a hard ride, a group of Double Circle riders who had escorted her into town reined back as she spat the words at him.

'Well, now, see here, Beth ...' he began.

'Little brother, you know nuthin' 'bout women!' Beth's tongue lashed him. 'Why, I do believe all this sleuthin's done gone to your head. You blind fool! Tom's right. Janelle is in danger. Kroll's double-crossed us all – includin' Janelle. She was plumb crazy about him. One thing's certain, she'll never get away from him if you don't do somethin' about it. She's family, Brad. You want it she should become an outlaw's woman? An' what about Elaine Rossiter? You gonna let Kroll get away with that? Now dust the seat of your pants, boy, and finish the job!'

'Now wait a minute ...' Brad began.

'Don't jest stand there, you're a Texas Ranger! Go take that gang apart!' she goaded him.

Beth was her old self, there was no denying the anger that blazed in her eyes as she held her skitting horse firmly in control. Aware of the grinning faces of the Double Circle riders, Brad knew further argument was useless. He swung into the saddle.

'I guess I'll ride with yuh,' Crellin said.

'Guess you'll need a gun, Boss.' One of his men flipped him a Colt. Crellin checked it was loaded, holstered it and swung up into the saddle.

'I guess I owe you an apology, Art,' Brad said as they rode towards the station. 'I was right out of order not tellin' you 'bout Elaine.'

Crellin shrugged. 'I guess she never thought anything much about me,' he said gruffly.

Brad drew his horse to a halt. 'That's not the impression I got,' he said quietly. 'She rated you above all the rest.'

The two men's eyes met in a look of mutual regard.

'Now, let's go get those guys,' Brad muttered between clenched teeth.

As they neared the train depot, they were stopped by a small group of Crellin's men. 'Don't stick yore head round that corner, Boss, or you'll lose it,' one of them said. 'Those guys mean business.'

At that moment the mournful sound of a siren told of the approaching train.

'So they're gonna hijack the train and grab the money,' Brad muttered.

'Maybe we should wire the authorities in Austin?' Crellin suggested.

Brad shook his head. Suddenly all his doubts fell away. He worried about Janelle; she was a city-bred lady, not as tough as Beth. 'They won't ride that far. Even if they did, Kroll will keep Mrs Hawk hostage fer as long as it takes.'

'So what'll we do?'

'As I see it, we can't stop them leavin' San Pedro. But if there was some way I could get on board that train, then maybe I can jump them when they're least expectin' it.'

Crellin looked concerned. 'Hell's teeth, is that wise?'

Brad shrugged. 'You think of anything better?'

'Cain't see how yore gonna do it,' Crellin muttered. 'Not here – the depot is too exposed to approach without being seen.' Suddenly he clicked his calloused fingers with a snap like a whiplash. 'North of here, the line takes a tight curve before the train crosses the bridge over the river. Then, fer about a country mile, the train never picks up beyond a walk until it gits to the far side and runs into open country.'

'You reckon we can make it there before the train?'

'Sure.'

By now the Double Circle riders had been reinforced with a strong contingent of armed citizens, incensed by what they had seen and heard.

'Listen!' Brad addressed them. 'Art an' me's taking care of this. Meantime, until the train leaves, I want the depot surrounding. I want as little bloodshed as possible so do nothing else, repeat nothing else, to provoke those guys, ya hear?'

There was a low growl of assent.

Brad turned back to Crellin. 'As soon as the train leaves, so do we.'

When Kroll and the outlaws arrived at the station, it was Levine who took charge. At his behest, Kroll herded Janelle together with a handful of would-be passengers at gun-point in the waiting-room while Levine and Billy Boy dealt with the incoming train.

'It's sure gone quiet out there,' Billy Boy remarked as he poked his Winchester round the corner of the waiting room and surveyed the deserted street beyond the warehouse.

'While ever we hold the woman, we're safe,' Levine said.

'Real smart aint'cha?' Billy Boy glanced in admiration at his companion as he spoke. 'I reckon you had somethin' like this figured all along.'

As the locomotive, belching smoke and steam, ground to a halt, Levine emerged from the deep shadow cast by the late afternoon sun to confront the engineer and fireman at gunpoint.

Levine held them, while Billy Boy mounted the first car and, brandishing his gun, cleared the two passenger cars, forcing the conductor and the score or so terrified passengers up the street.

'Must be a fair haul of wallets and watches, there,' Billy Boy observed, regretfully, as he watched them trudge away.

'Ferget it,' Levine snapped. 'There's more'n enough to be goin' on with inside that van.'

Levine pounded on the door of the express van with the butt of his rifle. When the door opened, he said to the messenger. 'Unlock the safe. Mrs Hawk's come to collect her money in person.'

Mindful of Levine's gun, the man did as he asked before he joined the occupants of the waiting-room.

'Looks like we're gonna get away with this,' Billy Boy crowed as he swung up into the express car. His eyes gleamed as he opened the safe door and held up a bundle of greenbacks for Levine to see.

'What did I tell ya?' Levine said. 'Stick with me an' you're gonna be rich. Now quit gloatin' and get those horses into the box car.'

Levine waited, his face impassive while Billy Boy took the fireman along to do his bidding.

When they were ready, Levine shouted to Kroll, who emerged from the waiting-room, pushing Janelle ahead of him.

'We may as well travel in comfort,' Kroll remarked as he pushed Janelle up in front of him into the first passenger car.

'I guess I'll guard the money,' Billy Boy said as he mounted the step of the express car.

Levine climbed into the cab with the engineer and fireman. He held his gun close to the head of the engineer.

'OK, now let's go us a little ways,' he snapped.

Brad rode hard after Crellin as the big foreman followed a narrow trail tracing the shortest distance across the shallow loop taken by the railway line.

After a while he became aware that he could hear the train chugging steadily along somewhere behind his left shoulder. He gave a sigh of relief for he had pinned all his hopes on Crellin's judgement and he wasn't going to be disappointed.

After half an hour's hard riding, Crellin signalled to slow down. He turned off the trail and threaded his way through the forest until they came to a shallow cutting carrying the railway on its final run in towards the bridge.

They reined in their horses and dismounted.

There was no need for them to press their ears close to the track and listen for the train, country-boy fashion, for they could see the plume of smoke hanging in the still air over the forest.

They hitched their horses to a nearby tree.

'We've only got the one chance to get on board,' Brad said as they took up position beside the track.

Crellin nodded and together the two men waited in tense expectation as the locomotive approached them. To Brad's satisfaction, it had slowed almost to a walk, just as Crellin had said.

Sweat ran down Crellin's face as the locomotive drew nearer. 'C'mon, baby, c'mon,' he prayed.

'Easy, now.' Brad stayed his companion's arm.

He was ice-cool now, seeing each move ahead clearly, as the locomotive trundled past them. His keen eyes picked out three men in the cab.

That accounted for one.

After the tender came the express car. Nothing visible, but one must be in there, he reasoned.

Then came the first passenger car.

'Mrs Hawk's in there — sitting with Kroll, I reckon,' said Crellin.

Brad agreed. He waited as the second empty car came trundling past. As soon as the box car, taking up the rear, came into view, he jumped to his feet.

'Let's go!' he cried.

The two men leaped forward down the bank, gathering speed as they ran downwards, easily catching up with the box car. Brad made it first, pulling himself on to the platform at the back and turning immediately to help the heavily-built Crellin up after him. Brad eased round the car and peeked through a vent.

'Horses are in here,' he remarked. 'Looks like they got it all fixed. I reckon they're plannin' on stopping the train soon and makin' a run fer it.' He turned to Crellin, who was breathing heavily. 'You ready?'

The big guy nodded and Brad led the way, favouring his injured shoulder as he hoisted himself on to the roof of the box car. Again he lent Crellin a hand and then the two men began to crawl, one behind the other, along the roof of each car until they came to the one which contained Kroll and Janelle.

Here Brad paused. Crellin joined him, his face

pale from the swaying motion of the car. Ahead they could see the bridge across the river.

'Wait here,' Brad told Crellin. 'While I go deal with Levine.'

Crellin's massive hand squeezed Brad's arm. 'You take care, ya hear?'

Brad nodded and crawled forward until he could climb on to the tender which was stacked high with coal. Thick black smoke blew back from the stack, enveloping him, making his eyes run and his throat tickle, but it also served as a screen as he inched forward over the piles of rough hewn coal towards the cab.

When he arrived, Levine was standing with his back to him, gun raised, his eyes never leaving the two men in front of him. The fireman was busy shovelling fuel into the box. The engineer was leaning on his elbow peering out of the left hand side of the cab at the approaching bridge.

'Stop the train once you get across the bridge,' Brad heard Levine say.

Slowly and with infinite care, Brad crawled closer and closer to Levine. But just as he straightened up, his foot dislodged a large chunk of coal, sending it crashing down into the cab.

As Levine whirled round, Brad projected himself forward. In the narrow confines of the cab there was no room for manoeuvre and before Levine could trigger his weapon, Brad's body hit him full on, knocking him backwards.

What happened next Brad would never forget for the rest of his life for Levine's shriek of agony, as the flames inside the firebox enveloped his head, made his blood run cold. Out of sheer humanity, he attempted to haul the man clear of the consuming flames. The engineer and fireman did their best to help but it was too late, for apart from the blazing horror wrought by the flaming furnace, Levine's neck had been broken by the impact against the grate.

'I cain't stop until we get over the bridge,' the engineer croaked as Brad displayed his badge of office.

Brad nodded grimly as the fireman dumped Levine's charred corpse on the tender.

Brad left the cab and retraced his steps back over the tender. As soon as the hunched figure of Crellin came into view, he gave the thumbs-up sign.

'Levine's dead,' Brad told him. 'The engineer's gonna stop the train once it's over the bridge. We're gonna release Mrs Hawk before we deal with Billy Boy. Now here's how we do it ...'

Crellin listened in silence as Brad outlined his plan. Then he began to work his way back along the roof until he reached the far end of the car.

Brad waited until he had done so, and then dropped down on to the platform at his end. With Crellin in position, he leaned round the end of the car and gave him the thumbs up.

Brad placed his hand on the door handle and began counting under his breath.

'Five, four, three, two one – GO!'

FIFTEEN

As the train jerked into motion and began to leave San Pedro, Janelle glanced about her and wrinkled her nose with distaste. Two rows of reversible seats separated the central aisle of the car. Brass kerosene lamps hung in the high clerestory roof. An unlit stove stood at one end; at the other end there was a door leading to a small lavatory. The air still carried the stale odour of those who had recently had their journey forcibly interrupted in San Pedro.

Kroll noticed her glance. 'Sorry I couldn't arrange a Pullman for you,' he said with a sarcastic grin.

The train gathered speed and when she didn't reply, he said, 'I guess I got it all wrong, Janelle, you'd've been worth a helluva sight more'n fifty grand when it comes to negotiatin'.'

'Do you really think you're going to get away with this tomfoolery?' Janelle said angrily. 'Why, every lawman in the land will be on the look-out for you.'

Kroll smiled. 'It's big country. Anyhow, what's the use of you protestin'? The way you helped me to get away back there is gonna convince that ranger that we're in this together.'

'You think you're real smart, don't you?' Janelle said angrily. 'To think I was taken in by you! I didn't believe a word the ranger was saying until you met up with those two hoodlums out in the street.' She shuddered. 'The way that young boy looks at me gives me the creeps.'

'Pay no mind to Billy Boy. I guess I'm as smart as you're good-lookin',' Kroll replied with a smirk.

He tried to take Janelle by the hand, but she snatched it away.

'Don't touch me!' she exclaimed.

'OK, OK, I got all the time in the world, now, I guess.' Kroll settled back in his seat with a smile.

'It wasn't necessary for you to murder Elaine,' Janelle said bitterly. 'She was a good friend to Beth.'

'She knew too much,' Kroll said harshly. 'I put her in a position of trust and she betrayed me.'

Janelle stared at Kroll as if he had just crawled out from underneath a stone. 'Trust? What do you know about trust? I trusted you as much as any man I've ever known. Look at how you've deceived me ...'

'Sure, sure,' Kroll placated her. 'So what's a few white lies when a guy falls for a woman? Face it, Janelle, if I'd pulled this off, you'd have married me before long.'

'Married you!' Janelle's voice rose over the clack and rattle of the bogies. 'That really is rich! You expect me to believe you did all this because you loved me? Why, all you ever wanted was to gain control of my money and humiliate my brother. To think, you could have ended up the boss of the

Double Circle!'

'Ain't nuthin' wrong with a little ambition,' Kroll replied.

'Sure,' Janelle agreed. 'My Wilbur used to say that. But he never did anyone any harm.'

They lapsed into an uneasy silence for the next few minutes as the train settled to a steady twenty miles an hour. Kroll put Crellin's Colt on the seat and settled back in his seat.

But Janelle couldn't rest. 'How are you gonna get out of this?' she said suddenly. 'Surely the authorities will be waitin' for the train when it arrives in Austin?'

Kroll pulled the brim of a stolen stetson down over his eyes and grinned. 'Sure they will, but when they check out this car they ain't gonna find anyone inside. We brought fresh horses along with us – we'll have long since gone. Best thing you can do is quit worrying and start thinkin' about adaptin' to life on the run fer a while.'

Janelle spent the next few minutes pondering the prospect of life as a fugitive with Kroll and his men. If Kroll was right, Tom would believe the ranger's story and would be thinking the worst of her by now. The only way she could convince him otherwise would be to ensure that these two men were delivered into the hands of the law. But how?

Kroll fell into a doze. As the train moved steadily on through the forest, Janelle studied the gun out of the corner of her eye. City bred and raised, she knew nothing of weapons. In her short stay out west she had marvelled at the casual way sidearms were worn by many men. Even her sister-in-law, Beth, was adept with a rifle. One day when they had been out riding she had shot and skinned a rabbit with casual ease – but Beth was a countrywoman and accepted such things as part of life.

The more Janelle looked at the gun, the more she realized it would be utterly useless for her to lean across Kroll and make a grab for it. Even if she succeeded, what good would it do to hold him at gunpoint if she didn't know how to fire the weapon? And even if she could shoot Kroll, the other two men were still at large on the train.

A feeling of hopelessness crept over her as she looked out of the window at the forbidding forest. Even if she managed to escape she could never hope to survive unaided in this wilderness. She shuddered. If Kroll were dead, her life would be worth nothing to the other two men when they had already taken possession of her money.

She winced at the irony of her situation. She had tried to end Tom's misery by ransoming Beth, only to end up a prisoner with the same evil men – and with no one to champion her cause ...

A slight noise disturbed her reverie. Suddenly she became alert for the noise seemed divorced from the rhythm of the motion of the car. In fact, it seemed to come from somewhere above her. She glanced upwards. Again she heard the soft scrabbling noise. She looked sideways at Kroll, but he had noticed nothing; he was sound asleep.

The scrabbling noise came again – this time further along the roof.

Janelle frowned. Was it a rat? Surely rail cars didn't have vermin. She looked round intently, but could see nothing.

She waited, listening intently for several minutes. Hearing nothing more she gave up and lay back and closed her eyes.

Suddenly she awoke with a start. There it was again! She froze, listening intently once more. There was no mistaking it, she could hear the same soft scrabbling noise again.

But this time it was going in the reverse direction!

Suddenly it dawned on her: *someone was moving along the roof of the car!*

A surge of hope rose inside her. She had seen Levine go into the cab; Billy Boy had gone into the express car ...

So whoever was moving above her wasn't a member of the gang!

She glanced again at the Colt lying on the seat between herself and Kroll. As she did so, the door of the car she was facing burst open and a man appeared pointing a gun ...

'Hold it right there!' Brad shouted.

He caught a glimpse of Janelle's pale face peering anxiously over the top of the seat. Behind her, at the far end of the car, the bulky figure of Crellin filled the doorway.

Kroll woke with a start and made a grab for his weapon, but Janelle had already leaned across him and made a snatch for it. There followed a short, sharp struggle during which Brad held off, helpless, lest the weapon discharge and Janelle be injured.

Kroll struck Janelle a savage blow and

recovered the Colt. He flourished it in triumph. 'Nothin's changed!' he shouted at Brad. 'I still have the woman. Now just drop your gun.'

Brad tossed his weapon on to a seat. 'You won't get away with this, Kroll,' he said.

Even as he spoke, Crellin was making his way stealthily down the aisle, from the opposite direction, his Colt in his hand.

Kroll laughed, unaware of Crellin's approach. He was brimming with arrogance now. 'So how are you gonna stop me?' he sneered.

Crellin was so close by now, he was able to reverse his weapon and raise it with the intention of smashing it down on the unsuspecting Kroll's head.

But as he did so, Janelle made a frantic effort to break loose. Kroll swung her round and faced Crellin who held off, afraid of hitting the woman. Brad snatched up his Colt and raced the last few yards down the aisle that separated him from Kroll.

Kroll discarded Janelle as easily as if she were a rag doll. She screamed as he levelled his gun at Crellin and fired. At short range, the effect of the .44 slug was devastating and Crellin was knocked over backwards. Leaving Janelle on the floor behind him, Kroll ran for the door by which Crellin had entered.

Blocked by the prone bodies of Janelle and Crellin, Brad, who had recovered his Colt, was forced to pause and pick his way over them.

But just as Kroll reached the door, the driver applied the Westinghouse brakes and the train slowed, throwing Brad off-balance. By the time he

Vacation at San Pedro 153

had recovered, Kroll had disappeared through the door, leaving it open behind him.

Brad raced after him with giant strides. The train was slowing and he arrived at the open platform on the end of the car just in time to see Kroll swing down onto the track side and break into a run towards the end of the train.

'Stop, Kroll, you ain't got nowhere to go!' Brad shouted.

Kroll was thirty yards away by now. He turned and raised his Colt, but the range was too great for any other than an expert marksman and his first – and only shot splintered the woodwork of the coach, a yard clear of Brad's head.

Colt already in hand, Brad had no compunction in returning the shot. Kroll dropped his weapon, slapped both hands to his heart as the slug hit home and slowly sank to his knees.

Brad wasted no more time on Kroll, for the train had come to a halt. He holstered his gun, turned and raced forward to the express car. As he arrived, the door slid open and a puzzled Billy Boy peered out.

'What's with all this screamin' an' shootin'?' he demanded.

His face changed when he saw Brad standing below him on the trackside.

'Levine's dead, so is Kroll. It's all over, Billy Boy,' Brad said. 'Quit while you're still alive.'

'No way!' Billy Boy shouted, 'I've still got the money in here – all fifty grand.'

He dropped into a gunfighter's crouch, his hands hovering over the butts of his Colts.

'Give yourself up, Billy Boy,' Brad said evenly.

'I killed a man in Austin,' Billy Boy bragged. 'I can kill you, too.'

Brad did not reply. Inside he knew there was no reasoning with the kid. Like dozens of others, he was in too far. Backing down meant losing face and Billy Boy was no coward.

A massive calm came over Brad. He was under no illusions. These raw youngsters could be lightning fast on the draw, but they lacked that vital sense of anticipation that comes with years of gunfighting.

In the ensuing moments, as their eyes locked, Brad detected a slight twitch in one of Billy Boy's facial muscles – a sure sign of the nervousness which inexperience brings.

'Draw, damn you, draw!' Billy Boy's voice rose to a screech.

But still Brad faced him, rock steady, balanced evenly on the balls of his feet, his right hand poised for the cross-draw.

As the final seconds of tension ticked inexorably away, Billy Boy cracked.

Even as his opponent's hands tensed, Brad's right hand was on its way, palming his weapon even as Billy Boy clawed at the butts of his own. Yet Brad could take no chances; Billy Boy had instigated a chain of events which caused his death long before the slug from the Colt slammed into him, doubling him over, forcing him to topple head first off the side of the express car on to the side of the track.

As Brad turned away, Crellin appeared, trailed by the engineer and fireman.

Janelle appeared on the platform of the car,

her pale face strained with anxiety. 'Brad, are you all right?' she called softly.

When he saw the prone form of Billy Boy, Crellin leaned against the side of the car and mopped his brow. 'Jeez, I heard you rangers were a bunch of hell-raisers,' he croaked. 'An' now I surely believe it.'

The evening was warm and sultry and the square dance in the barn at the Double Circle was reaching its climax.

As Brad took the air in the yard, he paused to roll a smoke, smiling to himself as the band played their hearts out, the fiddler scraping away to the pounding rhythm of a clevis and pin. The insistent sing-song voice of caller rang out the old familiar foot-tapping rhymes:

*'Choose your partner, form a ring,
Double eight and Double C swing.*

*First swing six, then swing eight,
Swing 'em like yore swingin' on a gate.*

*Ducks in the river, a-goin' to the ford,
Coffee in a little rag, sugar in a gourd.'*

There was a rustle and as he looked up, in the flare of the match, Brad saw a woman approaching him.

It was Janelle.

'What's this? Enjoying your own company?' she said.

Brad smiled. These last few days he had seen

rather a lot of Janelle – thanks to the Machiavellian scheming of big-sister, Beth. Long rides during timeless, sunlit days on the range followed by candlelit dinners in the evening had been instrumental in a softening up process it had been hard to resist.

Janelle slipped her arm in his and he walked her slowly away from the house. The nearness of her made his nerves tingle.

'Ain't this weather just perfect?' Janelle unconsciously mimicked a Texas drawl as they leaned over the corral fence and gazed out onto the range. 'I sure do like it out here in the west.'

'Even after what Kroll did to you?'

She shivered. 'We got hoodlums like him back east,' she said. 'I guess I'll never be able to thank you enough for saving me from him.'

Brad bit his lip at the irony of her remark. If it hadn't been for Beth's roasting he might have let her go with Kroll ...

Out on the range a coyote howled. A gentle breeze blew, carrying a potpourri of smells as fragrant as the woman standing beside him. As she came closer to him, he looked up and saw the sky was shot so full of stars it was as if someone had let loose at the heavens with both barrels of a shot-gun loaded with buckshot.

'I'm so pleased they've made Tom mayor,' Janelle said. 'He'll make San Pedro a place fit for decent folk to live in. I reckon he should go for state office, one day, don't you?'

'Sure,' Brad replied. He finished his cigarette and ground it out with his heel. 'I guess I never thought I'd come to terms with carpetbaggers, but

Tom's different. He's made Beth happy; I'm real pleased 'bout that.'

'I guess I'm a carpetbagger, too, Brad,' Janelle teased him.

She stood on tiptoe and kissed him.

Brad ran his fingers through her hair. This beautiful woman disturbed him profoundly. Tom had been dropping hints about needing more help with the ranch now that he had become mayor. A few more days of this gentle persuasion and he would succumb to the good life completely.

'Waal, I guess I did no more than my job,' he said. He took her arm again. 'Look, I guess we'd better get back inside, otherwise, folk will start talkin'.

'I think they already are,' Janelle replied.

Beth appeared in the doorway as they approached.

'Ah, there you are!' Her face broke into a knowing smile as she recognized them. 'Now what have you two been up to, I wonder?'

Brad was spared further embarrassment as Tom limped up behind Beth. 'By the way, Brad. A telegram came for you late this afternoon.' He fumbled in his vest pocket. 'You were out ridin' with Janelle and I was so busy with tonight's celebration, I guess it went clean outa my head.'

Conscious of the ring of eyes on him, Brad tore open the envelope and took out the message. He struck a match and read:

Hope you enjoyed vacation. Need you urgently back at HQ. McNelly.

'Anything wrong Brad?' asked Tom anxiously.

Brad smiled and shook his head.

111